I0531543

Buffalo Soldier:
The Lost Expedition

Charles Ray

Uhuru Press

This is a work of fiction. Names, places, organizations, and events are either fictional, or are used fictitiously. Any similarity to persons, living or dead, organizations or events completely coincidental.

No part of this book may be reproduced or distributed by any means or in any form, with the exception of fair use quotes in conjunction with editorial reviews, without the express written consent of the author.

For information about this book, or any other books by this author, visit the author's website at http://www.charlesray-author.com/

The author may be contacted through Uhuru Press at
charlesray.author@gmail.com.

Cover design by the author.

Manufactured in the United States of America.

Copyright © 2018 Charles Ray

All rights reserved.

ISBN: 0692052402
ISBN-13 978-0692052402:

DEDICATION

To all the soldiers who have served, who are currently serving, and who will serve in the future..

ACKNOWLEDGMENTS

The idea for this series about the Buffalo Soldiers was generated by the young people who served with me in the Foreign Service, who were unaware of the true history of the American West. I began writing these books to help fill in some of the knowledge gaps, and in the process learned a lot that even I, a student of U.S. military history, didn't know..

Chapter 1

The tinny notes of a bugle, playing First Call, echoed off the adobe walls of the barracks, yanking Ben Carter from the first sound sleep he'd had in two weeks. The quick notes told him, even in his half-awake state, that it was 5:30 in the morning, which, for the men of the Ninth Cavalry at Fort Union, meant that it was time to rise and shine. In half an hour, the bugler would sound Reveille, and every man at the fort would have to assemble for roll call, and then prepare for Stable Call, when they would have to report to the stables to feed and groom their horses before feeding themselves beginning at 6:30.

He groaned as he threw off the scratchy wool blanket and sat up, swinging his feet off the goose-down-filled mattress, and flinching when they came into contact with the chilled stone floor.

Through the door to the room he had to himself, due to his rank of field first sergeant, he heard the shuffling and murmuring of his men, also roused from sleep, and grumbling about it as soldiers have been doing, he thought, since the days of the Roman legions.

They would grumble, but they would comply. Their lives were ruled by those bugle calls; had been since the Americans had taken up arms against their English colonial masters a hundred years earlier. They'd thrown off English rule, but retained many of their former master's customs, the bugle calls being one in particular.

Developed in 1876, by Major Truman Seymour of the 5th U.S. Artillery, so that the entire army would have a standard system, the bugle calls regulated every hour of a soldier's day, regardless of rank or branch of service. Before the Civil War, the infantry had used drums, while the cavalry and artillery had used bugles, but after that conflict, the entire army had moved to bugles, which told a soldier what to do from the 'rise and shine' of First Call at 5:30 am until the 'lights out, time for bed' of Taps at around 9:30 pm.

Sitting on the edge of the bed, Ben pulled on his socks, pants, and boots. He grabbed his toothbrush and razor from the bedside table, and went out, through the main sleeping bay of the barracks, to the wash rack just outside the back door. His second in command, Sergeant George Toussaint, his suspenders flapping against his thighs, emerged from the nearby latrine. He smiled broadly as he saw Ben.

"Hey, Ben," he said. "How'd you sleep last night?"

Ben put his toiletries on the shelf near the water pump and headed toward the latrine. "Best sleep I've had in a while," he said. "How about you?"

"Not bad, but I coulda used a couple more hours."

"Yeah, tell me about it."

Ben entered the latrine, holding his breath against the smell that, despite liberal applications of lime, hung in the air like a wet, woolen blanket. He quickly emptied his bladder, and stepped back outside, waiting until he was back at the water pump to resume breathing deeply.

Toussaint laughed. "That there latrine's 'bout the only thing I don't miss about this place when we's in the field."

"Yeah, I wish they'd find a way to keep the smell down. Almost makes me want to be stopped up so I don't have to go." Ben pumped water into one of the basins lined up on the shelf, wet his brush and put some baking soda on it. He then vigorously brushed his teeth, something he also insisted that every man in his detachment do every day, even when in the field. After lathering up his face, he used his straight razor to hack off the small stubble that had developed since he last shaved two days earlier, rinsed off the remnant of lather, washed the rest of his face, and stowed his toiletries away.

Beside him, Toussaint had done the same, although, since his beard grew back at twice the rate of Ben's, it took him longer to shave.

"So, what's on our schedule for today?" Toussaint asked after he'd rinsed his face.

"After morning mess," Ben said. "We'll clean our field gear. Then, this afternoon, after noon mess, I think we should do some rifle drill, and maybe a little tracking."

"You gon' let Malachi and Hezekiah lead the rifle drill?"

"Yup, and Samuel will do the tracking."

Corporals Malachi Davis and Hezekiah Layton, and Sergeant Samuel Hightower, had been with Ben sine he'd been put in charge of M Troop's special operations detachment, back when the Ninth had been stationed in Texas. The two corporals were the youngest men in the unit, but were the best marksmen at Fort Union, while Hightower, who had been raised by an Indian tribe that had kidnapped him and his mother when he was still a baby, could find and follow a trail through rocky terrain, even when it had gone cold, and he moved as silently as a morning breeze through any kind of terrain.

"Do we really need extra training?"

Ben clapped his friend's shoulder. "Never hurts, George," he said. "Besides, it won't look right if everybody else is training, and we're not. You know Sergeant Major Oglethorpe would never stand for that. No special treatment while he's the top sergeant."

"Yeah, I s'pose you right. Okay, I'll go in and kick the rest out of their racks 'n we'll git the horses took care of, then see you in the mess hall."

"No, I'll see you at the stables. I don't believe in anybody getting special treatment either."

Ben made it a point to never send the men of his detachment to do anything he wasn't willing to do himself, and had done so since taking over the detachment when it's original commander fell ill. He was pretty sure they wouldn't hold it against him if he did like many of the other senior noncommissioned officers and let the junior soldiers do the dirty work, but he knew they respected him for pitching in. So, when Reveille sounded, he was there, front and center of his detachment, and then led them to the stable, where they saw to the detachment's mounts, eleven of the best horses at the fort. At 6:30, when the bugler sounded Mess Call, he led his men to the mess hall, and sat with them rather than in the section reserved for the senior sergeants, and then after mess, joined them in the main room of the barracks where they spent the rest of the morning cleaning and repairing their gear.

The detachment had just come back to Fort Union the day before, after a two-week reconnaissance mission southeast of the fort, near the settlement of Variodero, checking on reports of cattle rustlers operating in the area. They'd found nothing after ten days of sleeping rough, and being glued to their saddles for six to eight hours every day. Ordinarily, after a mission, the men would be given two or three days liberty, but since they'd not encountered any hostile action, Lieutenant Colonel Joshua Wainwright, commander of M Troop and Fort Union, had asked Ben to keep them at the ready. He hadn't said why, but Ben had learned that the officer usually had a good reason for what he did, so he didn't question his decision.

At noon, the detachment went to the mess hall for the midday meal. As they were leaving, on their way to the training ground on the east side of the fort, Sergeant Major Oglethorpe stopped Ben at the entrance to the building.

"First Sergeant Carter," he said. "Might I have a word with you?"

"Of course, sergeant major." Ben turned to Toussaint. "George, er, Sergeant Toussaint, you go ahead and take the men to training. I'll join you later."

Toussaint nodded, formed the detachment into two columns, and marched them smartly off.

"No need for the formality on my account, Ben," Oglethorpe said after the detachment had gone around the corner of the building. "I know you men operate pretty loose in the field, but it doesn't seem to affect your ability to get the job done."

"No, it doesn't, sergeant major, because my men all know their jobs, and everybody in the detachment respects everyone else. We don't need rank in the field. They know I'm in charge, so I don't need to remind them of it."

"I wish all the other sergeants on this post would think that way." Oglethorpe seemed to drift away from their conversation for a moment, as if he was lost in thought. Then, his sharp eyes turned back to Ben. "I need to talk to you about something important. Walk with me."

Without waiting for Ben to reply, he started walking across the post toward the officers' housing area. Ben quickly caught up and walked beside him, on his left as befitting one of junior rank.

"What is it you want to talk to me about, sergeant major?"

"You know . . . Ben . . . all the men in your detachment are corporals now."

Ben slowed, falling slightly behind Oglethorpe, and causing the man to slow his own pace to allow him to catch back up. "Yes," Ben said. "But, you know that, since you and the colonel presided over the last promotion, when Isaac Harris got his second stripe. Is that a problem?"

Oglethorpe stopped. Ben stopped and turned to face him, his face impassive.

"Yes, and no," Oglethorpe said. "There's no argument that Harris deserved the promotion. Hell fire, Ben, every man in your squad deserves the rank he has, and more." He hesitated, rubbing at his clean-shaven jaw. "It's just that some of the other sergeants are complaining about it."

"Why should my men's promotions be of any concern to the others?"

"They don't begrudge them getting promoted, Ben. The ten men in your detachment are the best soldiers at this fort, the best in the regiment for that matter. They're upset because all of 'em are in your unit, and not in theirs."

Ben felt a momentary stab of panic in his gut. He'd been in the army long enough to know the power wielded by the army's noncommissioned officers. Even in the black regiments, under the command of white officers, it was the sergeants, especially the senior men with years of experience under their belts, who actually ran things. If the other sergeants at Fort Union had their eyes on men in his detachment, it would be difficult to prevent them raiding him, unless he had the top sergeant at the fort on his side. For that reason, his next words were crucial.

"Are they pushing to have any of my men

transferred?" He held his hands behind his back, fingers crossed.

Oglethorpe's brow furrowed, and then smoothed out as he smiled. "Leave it to you to get right down to it. I like that. No, for now, it's just rumblings when they sit around the NCO quarters at night. Of course, it you didn't insist on bunking in with your men, you'd probably know that."

"I know I could get a room in the senior NCO building, but I find it better to stick close to the men. Considering some of the missions we get sent out on, I just feel like it's a good way to build the kind of teamwork we need to survive."

"Oh, I'm not criticizing you, son." Oglethorpe held his slender hands up in mock surrender. "I think you have the right idea. Just stating a fact, is all. Anyway, none of them have made any kind of official request, but it's just a matter of time before they do, so I thought you ought to be warned."

Ben breathed a sigh of relief. At least Oglethorpe was on his side—for now.

"So, sergeant major, what do you think I should do?"

"You know what they say. A good offense is the best defense."

Ben looked confused, and Oglethorpe laughed.

"Boy, for all your experience in the field, you still haven't mastered strategy, have you? You know that anyone wanting to get a man transferred has to come to me first, and then I tell the colonel who makes the final decision."

"I know that," Ben said.

"But, if the colonel already knows about it, because, say, you just happened to bring up how important it is to keep your squad just the way it is, and then I say I don't think making the transfer is such a good idea . . . well—"

"He'll turn the request down," Ben said, cutting him

off. "Sorry, to interrupt you, sergeant major, but I think I see what you mean. The side that attacks first has the advantage."

"You might just make a good sergeant major one of these days, Ben." Oglethorpe smiled wolfishly. "You just have to learn the play the politics of the army."

"Thank you for the heads up, sergeant major. Now, if you don't mind, I need to get back to my men."

Oglethorpe nodded, but as Ben turned back toward the training field, a corporal ran up to them, stopped, and bent at the waist to catch his breath. "S-sergeant major, f-first s-sergeant C-carter," he said. "The c-colonel want to talk to the b-both of you in his office."

"What about, soldier?" Oglethorpe asked.

"He don't say, s-sergeant m-major, he just tell me to go fetch you."

Oglethorpe shrugged, and turned to Ben. "Guess your men are gonna have to wait a bit, first sergeant," he said. "You and I have to go see the colonel."

Chapter 2

When the commanding officer summons, enlisted men, regardless of rank, do not dally. Ben and the sergeant major walked briskly across the fort, turning right when they came to the street in front of the row of officers' housing, and made their way to the headquarters building.

Lieutenant Colonel Joshua Wainwright sat behind his desk, picking at his mustache. Sitting nervously on the edge of a chair to the right of the desk, a man who looked to be in his early thirties, wearing a dark gray suit, with a bowler hat on his lap, fidgeted.

Ben and Oglethorpe stopped in front of Wainwright's desk, came to attention and saluted.

"Sergeant Major Oglethorpe and First Sergeant Carter, reporting as ordered," Oglethorpe said.

Wainwright nodded at them. "Thank you for coming gentlemen." He waved at two chairs sitting against the wall to the left. "Take a seat, please."

After they were seated, the room fell quiet. Ben's attention was drawn to the man seated across the width of the desk from him. Something about the man, and his nervous manner, his slack-jawed expression, the way he kept his gaze on the tips of his boots, and constantly fidgeted with his hat, worried him.

Wainwright looked from his two sergeants to the man, furrowed his brow, then tugged at his mustache again before speaking.

"You two are probably wondering why I wanted to see you," he said. "I'd like to introduce Mr. James Heatherton, from Albuquerque. He has a story to tell that I want you to listen to first, and then I'll explain what I want from you."

For the first time, the man looked up and at them, an expression on his face as if he was just noticing their presence.

"My father," he said. "Is William Randolph Heatherton. He owns the El Dorado Silver Mine, not the largest, but one of the richest in the Albuquerque area." He continued to play with his hat as he spoke. "He is also something of an amateur scientist, specializing in geology and anthropology.

He stopped talking, stopped rotating the hat, and looked at Ben and Oglethorpe. When his gaze locked with Ben's, he held it for a few heartbeats, and for the first time since he'd entered the room, Ben saw something akin to emotion. But, he couldn't identify the emotion.

"For the last few years," Heatherton continued. "My father has left the running of the mine to me. He has devoted most of his time to pursuing a theory he has about the Anasazi."

"What is the Anasazi?" Ben asked.

"Please, don't interrupt, first sergeant," Wainwright said, looking sternly at Ben.

"Oh, that's perfectly all right, colonel," Heatherton said. "I can understand the sergeant's curiosity. Three years ago, I would have been just as confused. But, for that period of time, it's just about all my father has talked about."

Wainwright looked at him, some of the sternness

leaving his expression. "Well, in that case, what *is* an Anasazi, Mr. Heatherton?"

"Anasazi is not an *it*, colonel, but a *who*. The Anasazi are believed to be the original native inhabitants of much of northern New Mexico Territory, Arizona, Colorado, and Utah. They were cliff dwellers, and are thought to perhaps be the ancestors of the Hopi. Supposedly, they occupied this area over a thousand years before the birth of Christ, and had large, sophisticated cities, irrigation canals, and roads. Some ruins have been found in the northwest part of the territory, but they pose more questions than answers. You see, several hundred years ago, the Anasazi vanished, disappeared without a trace except for a few pueblos in the sides of cliffs, and some fragments of pottery."

Wainwright shook his head, and tugged at his mustache. "You mean, they were gone before the first white men came to this continent?"

"That's correct." Heatherton nodded. "Except for the few cliff dwellings, it's as if they never existed."

"If that's the case, how do we even know they existed in the first place? I mean, the Hopi are cliff dwellers. Maybe the pueblos that were found belonged to them."

"No, my father and others have talked with the Hopi and some of the other tribes, and they all say that these structures were built by the 'old ones.' The name, Anasazi, by the way, is Navajo, and means 'enemy ancestors.' The Hopi word for them is 'Hisatsinom,' but, that's a hard word for most whites, who use the Navajo word."

Ben continued to look confused, wondering where this story of some old Indian tribe was going, and what it had to do with the cavalry, but Wainwright had ordered him to hear the man out, so he would bite his tongue and wait for him to get to the point of his story.

Heatherton seemed to be unaware of how boring his

story was as he continued. "As I said, the Anasazi just disappeared. No one knows why, but my father thinks they migrated, and that the logical direction for them to go was east. Four months ago, he organized an expedition to examine his proposition. The first place he decided to look was the Sangre de Cristo Mountains, on the theory that, as cliff dwellers, the Anasazi would've moved through mountains on their trek. He hoped to find evidence of their presence in these mountains, and perhaps indications of where they went from there."

Then, he simply stopped talking, and his gaze dropped back to the tips of his boots.

"Well, First Sergeant Carter," Wainwright said. "You've been sitting there looking like you want to ask a question, so now's your chance."

Ben cleared his throat.

"Yes sir, colonel. I guess the first question I have is, what does any of this have to do with the army?"

Wainwright half smiled and looked from Ben to Oglethorpe.

"I'm with Ben on this, sir," Oglethorpe said. "This is all interesting, but I don't see what it has to do with the Ninth."

Wainwright's smile was now in full beam.

"Good point, gentlemen, very good point," he said. "That's why I asked for you, Ben. You see, the story you've just heard has *nothing* to do with the army. It's what Mr. Heatherton asked me before you came that's important, but I wanted you to hear the full story so you'll know what you're about to be sent into. Now, Mr. Wainwright, will you please tell Sergeant Carter here just what you want from the army?"

"Yes, thank you, colonel. Gentlemen, as I said, my father and his party came to the Sangre de Cristo Mountains four months ago. He sent a few telegrams from Cimarron during the first two months, mostly reporting that they'd found nothing. Then, two months ago, he sent a telegram saying that they'd found something interesting. That was the last telegram. I went to Cimarron and asked around, and the telegraph office said that was the last message he sent. No one else in town recalls seeing either him or anyone from his party for two months now."

Ben sat forward in his chair. "So, you think he's lost in the mountains?"

"Yes, I do, sergeant, and I'd like the army to help me find him."

Charles Ray

Chapter 3

After Wainwright confirmed that he was assigning the mission of finding James Heatherton and his party to Ben's detachment, Ben left him, Heatherton's son, and Sergeant Major Oglethorpe in Wainwright's office, and jogged to the training field. He'd decided that it was best to depart on the mission right away rather than wait until the next day, and it only took him a few minutes to explain this to his men. Within an hour, the detachment was packed and mounted, along with three pack animals, and waiting outside the headquarters building for William Heatherton to finish saying his thanks and goodbyes to the colonel.

Ben's sense of unease about him was immediately reinforced when, after informing Heatherton that they would go first to Cimarron, the man disagreed with him in front of his detachment.

"I've already spoken to people there," he said. "It would be a waste of time. We should proceed directly to the mountains."

Ben took a deep breath to control his emotions.

"Mr. Heatherton, it's never a good idea to go into an

area until we know all we can about it. When you were in Cimarron, did you get an exact location of your father's camp?"

Heatherton's face reddened. "Uh, no, I didn't. Why is that important?"

"If we go directly to the mountains, we could waste a few days trying to find it. If we know where he camped, we might be able to pick up a trail. Otherwise, we'd be going in blind."

"Oh, yes, I see," Heatherton said, but with little conviction in his voice. "Yes, I suppose it is wiser to start in Cimarron. Very well, shall we proceed?"

"You can ride up alongside me," Ben said.

When Heatherton pulled his horse up on Ben's left, Ben said nothing, but he pulled his horse back and around, and moved up on Heatherton's left. He then raised his hand and signaled the detachment to move out.

As they rode away, over his shoulder, Ben noticed Wainwright and Oglethorpe standing on the porch of the headquarters building, watching with broad smiles on their faces. Well enough for them to smile, he thought. They don't have to deal with this obnoxious, rich greenhorn for who knows how long. He took a deep breath and turned his head forward.

They took the road north toward Raton, on the border with Colorado, and just before the road reached the Canadian River, they turned left toward the Sangre de Cristo Mountains. The smaller road ran past a number of small farms before reaching Cimarron, a small town at the foothills of the mountains.

The sun was just dipping toward the western horizon by the time they reached the outskirts of the town. Ben inquired of an old man on the sidewalk in front of the general store about the location of the town livery stable, and was told that it was at the western outskirts. They rode through a town that was just beginning to get ready for the influx of cowboys and miners visiting one of the town's three saloons. Ladies in long dresses, their heads covered by bonnets, were rushing to get home before the main street was overrun by men drunk, or on their way to get drunk, who might assume that any woman out after dark was one of the entertainers from one of the saloons. The town's bank was already dark and shuttered, and the general store was being closed as they talked to the old man. By the time the detachment reached the livery stable, the only establishments left open were the livery stable, the three saloons, the hotel, and the sheriff's office.

The livery stable owner, a grey-haired, gnarled old man with teeth stained brown from the plug of tobacco that he constantly chewed, welcomed them, and offered good rates to stable their horses and provide storage space for the larger items of their supplies.

While the men were grooming the horses prior to putting them in stalls, Ben pulled the old man aside.

"We're here to look for some people who were planning on exploring the mountains," he said.

The old man hawked a brown globule of spit at the straw floor of the stable. "You must be talkin' 'bout that greenhorn, Heatherton, and his crew," the man said. Ben nodded. "Well, ain't heard nothin' from 'em fer nigh on to six week now. Heatherton used to come to town 'bout once a week, 'n he allus kept his horse 'n mule here."

"Do you have any idea what might have happened to them?"

"Naw, but that part of the mountains they was plannin' on goin' to is s'pose to be hainted. Somethin' 'bout old Injun spirits or somethin' like that. All I know is ain't nobody 'round here'd dare go up there.'

Heatherton came over to them just as the man was speaking.

"These Indians, would they be Anasazi?" he asked.

"Yeah, that sounds like what they call 'em, why?"

"Because, my father was trying to prove that the Anasazi lived in this area."

"Well, they don't live here now," the old man said. "Ain't fer the fifty years I been livin' here, and not fer the time my pa lived here. We been in these here parts fer near on to sixty-five years. They's stories 'bout some old Injuns what lived in caves up in the mountains, but they done died out more 'n a hundred years ago, I heard."

Heatherton and Ben shared a look.

"Do you know where they went exactly?" Ben asked.

"Well, not perxactly, but I kin draw you a map that'd show you close to where they went."

"I'd appreciate that."

"It's gon' take me a while. I'll give it to you in the mornin'."

Ben thanked him, payed the deposit of four dollars he requested, and turned to leave. At the entrance to the stable, Heatherton stopped him, and proffered his hand.

"Sergeant, I owe you an apology," he said. "You were right to come here first. When I visited here, I never thought to ask for specific directions to where my father and his people were. I just assumed I'd be able to find it."

"No apologies necessary," Ben said. He shook the man's hand, but his doubts about him weren't quite allayed. "Now, we need to get rooms for the night and find a place to get some supper."

"I know the owner of the hotel," Heatherton said. "So, we'll have no problems there. As for supper, I believe there are two choices, the saloon across the street from the hotel, or the dining room of the hotel itself. Frankly, while the rooms in the hotel are clean enough, I didn't find the food all that good."

"Then, I reckon we'll eat at the saloon." Ben had preferred that option anyway, considering the possibility of gathering more information would be greater in a drinking establishment where ears are plentiful and tongues loose.

True to his word, Heatherton talked the owner of the hotel into providing them with seven rooms, with the men of the detachment sleeping two to a room, and Ben and Heatherton assigned private rooms, at a rate of a dollar per night. Eleven dollars took a large chunk out of Ben's traveling funds, but still left him a sufficient amount to buy supplies should they be needed. After securing their weapons in the room to be occupied by Toussaint and Hightower, and assigning Corporal Reuben Kincaid the duty of standing first guard, with Corporal Marcus Scott to relieve him after one hour, they went across the street to the saloon.

The place was noisy and crowded, but they managed to find two tables in the corner near the bar that accommodated them. A skinny, redheaded woman, with one molar missing, came to the table.

"What kin I git you gentlemen this evening?" she asked.

"What's good?" asked Toussaint.

"Well, we got steak and collard greens, or you can have fried chicken," she said.

"Do you have beef stew, baked Irish potatoes, and biscuits," Heatherton asked.

"We don't usually, hon," she said. "But I can have the cook rustle it up fer ya. We ain't had nobody order that since Mr. William et here."

Heatherton perked up. He reached out and grasped the woman's wrist. "Mr. William? Would you by any chance be referring to Mr. William Heatherton?"

She pulled her wrist away and frowned at him. "Yeah, that's his name. You know him?"

"Yes, I do. He's my father."

"For sure? You don't look nothin' like him."

"Be that as it may," Heatherton, tilting his head back and regarding her down the length of his nose.

"He *is* my father. When did you last see him?"

"You don't act nothin' like him, either. He's a nice man, and don't go grabbin' on people, or talkin' down to 'em."

Ben realized that the woman had identified what it was about Heatherton that he didn't like. The man had a sense of superiority over others, and wasn't at all hesitant to display it. In this case, though, it could cut off a possible source of useful information, something he wanted to avoid.

"You have to excuse him, ma'am," Ben said. "He truly is Mr. Heatherton's son, and he hasn't heard from him in two months, so he's a mite worried, that's why he seems a bit curt."

The woman smiled her thanks at Ben, and while she didn't smile at Heatherton, a faint look of sympathy crossed her face as she looked back at him. "I reckon I kin understan' that. If my pa was missin', I'd be a bit put out, too. Last time Mr. William was here was 'bout two months ago, I reckon. He was as jumpy as a young colt. Said he'd found a shard, or something like that, and that it would prove he'd been right all along. I ain't had no idea what he was talkin' 'bout, or what this shard thing is, but I tell you, he was a pure dee happy man that night. Ain't seen him since, though."

Heatherton looked at Ben. "That's the second person to tell us that my father hasn't been in town for two months."

Despite his distrust, and almost dislike for the man, Ben felt some sympathy for him when he saw the look of misery on his face. "You heard her, though. He found something important. Maybe he went deeper into the mountains to check on it, and just hasn't come back yet."

Heather shook his head. "No, even if he found an Anasazi site, he would still try to communicate with me. It's not like him to go so long without a telegram. I just know something's terribly wrong."

"Well, let's not get all het up until we know more," Ben said. "We'll head out first thing in the morning, to the area the livery man told us about, and work from there. In the meantime, let's get fed and get some sleep."

Ben and his men ordered steaks, while Heatherton insisted on the beef stew. When the woman brought the bowl of brown broth with large lumps of meat in it, Ben had to admit that it did smell good, but the steak she brought him was cooked just the way he liked it, dark brown, almost burned on the outside, and pink on the inside, and his collard greens had chunks of pork fat which added to the flavor. When everyone, including Kincaid, was fed, Ben ordered his detachment to hit the sack, and be prepared to ride at first light. They would be leaving before the hotel kitchen room served breakfast, so would eat cold rations on the trail, which caused Heatherton to grumble, but Ben held firm. The longer they delayed in town, the harder it would be to find a trail.

Heatherton was still grumbling the next morning when Ben roused everyone and they made the trek through the deserted streets to the livery stable. Finally, Ben could take no more of his carping.

"Look, Mr. Heatherton," he said. "Once we get in the mountains, there won't be any hotels or saloons, and sometimes we won't be able to have a fire. You'd better get used to eating cold rations, because, I don't know how many more time you'll have to do it until we find your father."

Heatherton mumbled something incoherent.

"It ain't too bad once you get used to it," Toussaint said. "Just wash it down with lots of water."

Ben turned away from the man and raised his hand. "All right, let's move out," he said. "We'll eat on the trail."

Ben rode with his shoulders straight, and his back

stiff, ignoring the man who rode at his side. As the sun rose behind them, he could feel its warmth on his back.

He had them ride at a leisurely walk to allow the man to eat their dry rations with one hand, while keeping the other on the reins. Out of the corner of his eye, he noticed that Heatherton, upon seeing how easy the soldiers accomplished the task of eating in the saddle, and their utter lack of complaint, managed to copy them, though clumsily at first, with increasing ease. When everyone had eaten, and washed the dry food down with swigs from their canteens, he had them settle into an easy canter, his aim being to reach the lower reaches of the mountains and the area where the livery man had said Heatherton senior had set up his base camp by mid-afternoon at the latest.

The relatively flat land around Cimarron changed no more than four miles west of the town, first to a kind of washboard pattern of small hills and dry washes, with sawgrass ground cover, and quickly turning into larger hills and hidden valleys, and large stretches of yellow-brown, rocky soil dotted with rocks and juniper trees. The hillsides were covered by black pine, juniper and burr oak trees. Settlements were few and far between, and as they neared the lower reaches of the Sangre de Cristo, they saw more and more wildlife; a few prairie dogs and jack rabbits, and as the hills got higher, antelope and mountain goats. The animals they saw were in small, scattered groups, except for the rabbits, which tended to be alone, and darted away whenever Ben's group approached them. The lone exception was a hawk perched on the branch of a burr oak tree that sat as still as a rock, only swiveling its head to watch them as they passed.

The noonday sun was beating down mercilessly by the time they arrived in the foothills proper, land marked by sharper elevations, larger rock formations, and fewer broadleaf trees.

As they neared the mountains, Ben had sent Hightower out ahead of the formation. His job was to try and locate the expedition's camp site based on the directions they'd been given. That meant he'd be riding a crisscross pattern, while the rest of the detachment would maintain a generally northwest course. When he found the location, he would turn back and find them, and then lead them there. Raised from infancy by the Kiowa Indians of north central Texas after he and his mother had been kidnapped from the farm where they'd been held as slaves, Hightower was the best tracker in the Ninth, and could find and follow a month-old trail when signs were invisible to the rest of the men in the unit.

Ben was just thinking that it was time to call a halt for the midday meal when he spotted the sergeant approaching them from the west. He raised his right hand to stop the column.

"Why are we stopping?" Heatherton asked.

"Sergeant Hightower's coming," Ben said. "That means he's probably found your father's camp site."

"Shouldn't we be moving on, then? We ought to be able to get there soon."

Ben fought the urge to raise his voice at the man. "First, we'll stop here and eat," he said, keeping his voice even. "Then, we'll move out. The way Sergeant Hightower's riding, I don't think he found anything that indicates that your father's in any immediate trouble. It'd be best if we were rested and nourished before we move on. Okay, men, dismount and get some grub going. We'll eat quick, and soon's we hear what Samuel has to say, we'll move out."

Ignoring Heatherton's frown, he dismounted and walked his horse to a stunted looking pine tree and tied it off.

Accustomed to moving quickly in the field, they had their horses tied off, a small fire going, and a pot of coffee brewing by the time Hightower reached them.

He dismounted, tied his horse next to Ben's.

"I found their camp site," he said as he walked up beside Ben. "But, it's been empty for at least a week or more."

"Any sign of trouble?" Ben asked.

"No, looks to me like they just packed up and left."

"Which way did they go?" Heatherton had walked up. He asked the question with a worried look on his face.

Hightower looked at Ben, who nodded for him to respond. "They went due west from the camp site, directly up into the mountains."

Chapter 4

They hadn't dawdled over the meal, and were quickly back in the saddle and, with Hightower leading the way, on their way to where he'd spotted the camp site. They arrived around the middle of the afternoon.

It didn't take a master scout to tell that someone had camped in the area for an extended period. A black circle in the red dirt indicated where they'd built their cook fire; the latrine pit, although filled in, could still be smelled from twenty feet away; and there were rectangles of brown vegetation and packed earth where the expedition had erected their tents.

Heatherton stomped around the area, though avoiding the latrine, casting wary glances at Ben and Hightower. Finally, he walked over to them and stood facing Hightower, his hands on his hips.

"How can you be so sure when they left here?" he asked.

Hightower looked at the man's florid face, his own expression as still as the surface of a mountain lake. When he spoke, his voice was quiet and even. "The grass where they set the tents is still beat down," he said. "If they been gone more'n a month, it would've growed back by now. I saw rabbit tracks near where they built the fire, and from the scat, I reckon them to be a week old. So, that means they left here more'n a week ago, but less'n a month. I'd guess closer to two weeks."

Heatherton looked skeptical.

"He knows what he's talking about," said Ben. "Sergeant Hightower was raised by Indians. He's just about the best tracker we got in the Ninth Cavalry."

"So, you can follow their trail, sergeant?"

Hightower rubbed at his chin. "I can't promise you nothin'," he said. "The trail's pretty clear from here, but the further we get up in the mountains, the harder it's gon' be to follow. But, I'll do my best."

The way Heatherton's eyes flickered, Ben was afraid he was about to start an argument, or worse, insult Hightower. Instead, the man looked at the sergeant with a slight smile on his face.

"Well, I guess if there's anyone who can find 'em, sergeant, it's you." He turned to Ben. "Are we ready to move out?"

"As soon as we finish eating," Ben said.

They made quick work of the midday meal, doused the fire, and were back in the saddle within an hour. With Hightower twenty yards in front, and Heatherton riding beside Ben, they headed northwest toward a cut in the hills.

Soon, they were well into the lower reaches of the mountains, following a narrow track between towering rock faces that rose a hundred feet above them in places. Gnarled trees, bent and twisted by the wind as they grew, jutted out of the sides. The trail cut an irregular path, ever upward, narrowing in some places so much that they were forced to ride single file. In some ways, it was no different than many of the other mountain trails they'd trekked, but for some reason, the way the crunch of the horses' hooves on the rocky ground echoed off the rock walls caused Ben to glance from side to side. It felt to him as if they were being watched by unseen eyes from the narrow ridges that lined the gray rock walls.

Up ahead, Ben noticed that Hightower was moving slowly, leaning over his horse's neck and peering at the ground. What he was seeing, Ben could only guess, for he himself saw no signs of the expedition's passage on the rough ground beneath his horse's hooves.

Their pace slowed even more as they entered the elevation where larger trees were replaced by stunted evergreens and there was more rock than dirt. The trail alternated between narrow and wide, and continued upward in a series of switchbacks that sometimes slanted downward so that the men in the back of the column could see Hightower below them, or upward, and they could see him by craning their heads back.

Ben noticed that Heatherton had gone quiet, and clung tightly to his horse's reins, his gaze darting from side to side as they transited the narrow spaces.

He began to worry himself as the lengthening shadows indicated late afternoon, and they still hadn't found a place suitable to set up camp for the night. The last thing he wanted to do was stop in a narrow stretch of trail that would force them to camp strung out in a long and vulnerable line.

Then, he came around a sharp turn in the trail, and found himself in a section that was over fifty yards wide between the sheer rock walls, and that was relatively level in a generally southeast to northwest direction that seemed to stretch out nearly a quarter mile. Up ahead, about two hundred yards distant, he saw that Hightower had dismounted and was kneeling, examining something on the ground.

He raised himself in the saddle and turned to address the men behind him. "We'll be setting up camp here for the night. George, set sentries, get the tents set up and send somebody out to gather firewood."

Toussaint touched a forefinger to the brim of his hat, turned and began issuing orders. Ben urged his horse forward toward Hightower. He could hear the clop of Heatherton's horse's hooves behind him.

They stopped a few yards from where Hightower was still kneeling, studying the surrounding ground.

"What you got?" Ben asked.

Hightower looked up, a worried expression on his face.

"Looks like they camped here," he said. He picked something up from the ground. "And, mebbe they left in a hurry."

He held up a cylindrical black object, which after a few seconds, Ben recognized as a spyglass. Heatherton, though, recognized it immediately.

"That's my father's," he said.

He got off his horse and approached Hightower, his hand outstretched. Hightower handed him the instrument.

"You sure this belong to your pa?" Hightower asked.

"No doubt about it," Heatherton said. He pointed to three parallel lines scratched into the black metal body of the telescope. "These are the marks he puts on all his equipment. This spyglass is a particular favorite of his."

Ben and Hightower shared a look.

"What do you think, Samuel?" Ben asked.

"It looks like it was dropped," Hightower said. He then pointed to a flat area off to his left, where Ben saw a dark circle indicating that a fire had been built. "Over yonder, beyond the fire, is a tent pole still in the ground. Looks like the tent was taken down pretty fast to me."

Heatherton looked puzzled. "What does that mean?" he asked.

Hightower stood, and turned slowly, surveying the

area. "From the way the ground's disturbed, I'd say they left in a hurry. Beyond that, I can't say."

"Can you find their tracks?" Fear and worry creased Heatherton's face.

"It might take a while, and it's gon' be dark soon. I might have to wait until morning to get a good look." As he spoke, Hightower smiled, but Ben could see that the smile didn't reach his eyes.

"Mr. Heatherton, why don't you go get your horse tied up and get some rest," Ben said. "We'll be getting an early start in the morning, and everyone needs to be rested."

Heatherton hesitated for a moment, and then nodded. "Yes, I suppose that would be a good idea." He turned and walked toward the rest of the men, who were busy setting up camp.

Ben watched him go, and when he was too far away to overhear, he turned back to Hightower.

"You have something on your mind, Samuel. What is it?"

"I didn't want to give him anything to worry 'bout, Ben. But, it looks to me like the folks who were in this camp didn't leave voluntarily."

"What makes you say that?"

Hightower pointed toward the darkened area where a fire had burned. "Well, for starters, they didn't douse the fire here like they did at the first camp."

Ben looked closely, and saw several unburned pieces of wood in the circle. At the first camp site, there had only been a blackened circle of ground.

"And, there's more 'n one tent pole left in the ground," Hightower continued. "Ain't likely they'd leave 'em if they struck the tents normally. It's like the tents was just yanked down."

Ben pondered what he was hearing. He felt a sensation at the nape of his neck like ants were crawling across his flesh.

"You think someone took 'em? Maybe, they were

just careless striking camp."

Hightower shook his head. "Naw, I don't think so, Ben. The ground's pretty hard, but I can see signs of more horses here than they had down below. No, somebody done took 'em, Ben."

"Can you find the trail?"

"Like I said, the ground's pretty hard, and the tracks are all mixed up. Come sunrise, I'll look around and see if I can figure which way they went when they left here."

Ben shook his head. "Who in blazes would want to kidnap a bunch of crazy people out looking for Indian signs?" he muttered.

"One thing's for sure," Hightower said. "Whoever it was, it wasn't Injuns."

"How do you know?"

"I know, 'cause all the hoof marks I saw was shod."

"Outlaws, maybe," Ben said. "Robbin' 'em?"

Hightower shook his head. "Been robbers, they'd of just stole their valuables and left 'em, or if they was a real bad bunch, kilt 'em and left their bodies for the buzzards. Naw, Ben, somebody done took 'em. This here Heatherton fella, was kinda rich, wasn't he? Maybe somebody done kidnapped him for ransom."

"I don't think so. Heatherton didn't say anything about getting a demand for ransom."

"You gon' ask him 'bout it?"

"Not just yet. Let's see if we can pick up a trail and see if we can figure out which way they went."

Chapter 5

At the first sign of dawn the next day, a graying of the sky overhead, they rose, prepared a quick breakfast, and while the men struck camp, Hightower mounted and began riding a circle around the camp sight, looking for the outbound trail.

About a hundred yards north of the site, he stopped and dismounted. After kneeling and examining the ground, he stood and waved.

"You find a trail?" Ben asked when they rode up to where he stood.

Hightower pointed north. "Yup. They went that way. I count twelve horses. How many with old man Heatherton?"

"My father had three people with him," Heatherton, who was riding next to Ben, said. "Henry Cabot, Meriwether Johnson, and Cady Logan. They would've had two pack horses. Why are there twelve horses?"

Ben hesitated for a few seconds, and then decided it was no use trying to conceal the information. "It means there were six people with them when they left here," he said.

It took a few seconds for Heatherton's brain to process that bit of information.

"Y-you think my father and his group were . . . kidnapped?"

"I'm sorry, Mr. Heatherton, but it sure looks that way. Can you think of anyone who would want to harm your father?"

Heatherton shook his head vigorously. "No. Everyone likes him. Oh, people who know him well, think he's not totally right in the head, what with his obsession with ancient Indian culture, but I know of no one who would wish him harm."

"Do you think someone might take him in order to get money from you or your company?"

Again, the head shake. "I suppose that's always a possibility, although, we are, despite the success of our business, not awash in cash. Most of the profits, since my father turned daily operations over to me, are put back into the business. Besides, if he was being held for ransom, why have I not been contacted by his abductors?"

Ben bit his bottom lip. Nothing about the situation was making sense. He turned slowly and surveyed the scene, especially the area in the vicinity of the blackened earth indicating where a fire had burned. While he could now see that Hightower had been right, it looked like the site had been hastily evacuated, there were no other signs of violence. No spent casings, no blood trails. If Heatherton and his party were taken, he thought, it was done quickly and with a minimum of violence. Of course, that didn't rule out the possibility that they'd been injured. Six men sneaking into the camp under cover of darkness might have been able to subdue an elderly man and three others without using guns or knives. But, there was still the nagging questions: who and why? Kidnappers would've demanded ransom by now, surely, and robbers, would've just killed them, stripped them of their valuables and rode on.

"What about the equipment he carried with him,"

Ben said. "Was any of it valuable? What about cash? Would he be traveling with a large amount?"

Heatherton rubbed his chin and closed his eyes. When he opened them, he said, "Except for some of his surveying equipment, which is pretty expensive, the most valuable things they had were the horses. I think, when he started the expedition, he had two thousand dollars cash for buying supplies, but a good bit of that would already have been spent by now."

Ben looked at Hightower. "Can you follow the trail, Samuel?"

The look Ben got from his friend was raised eyebrows and head tilted back, with lips turned slightly down. "Yeah, I can follow it," he said, turning and mounting his horse.

He turned his horse's head north and started out in a walk, bent over the animal's neck and peering at the ground.

"Kind of touchy fella, isn't he?" Heatherton said.

Ben shrugged. "Okay, everyone, mount up. We follow Samuel."

He let Hightower remain twenty to fifty yards in front of the column, closing the gap when the valley they were riding through began to wind in a ragged, zig-zag course. At places it widened out, allowing them to ride comfortable in two columns, and at others it was so narrow that the rock walls were close enough to touch. In one of the wide areas, the gray stone of the walls on the west had dark streaks where water flowing from the top had mixed with the minerals of the rocks, while on the east, there were irregular openings in the wall, up a good hundred feet from the valley floor. The dark openings were in pairs and looked like eyes gazing out over the valley. If not for the sheerness of the walls, with a lack of ledges wide enough for anyone to perch on, Ben would have been concerned about the possibility of an ambush. Even lacking that, though, he felt a chill throughout his body whenever he looked up at the openings.

As he looked up ahead at Hightower, stopping now and then to get a better look at trail signs, he wondered if he was feeling the same. While Ben didn't think of himself as superstitious, like believing in ghosts or anything, but, he'd long since learned to trust his instincts. And, right at that moment, his instincts were giving him an itch on the back of his neck. He wasn't sure what it was, but something wasn't right. He knew that Samuel Hightower often had similar feelings when things were about to go wrong, and he ached to find a quiet moment away from the others to ask him about it.

In the meantime, he would try and keep his unease from showing, especially to James Heatherton. Ben had still to warm up to the man, but that didn't keep him from wanting to avoid worrying him any more than was necessary.

So, he took a deep breath, squared his shoulders, and fixed his gaze on the ground in front of the column, and when he looked to the sides, tried to avoid looking up at the looming cliff walls, especially the ones with the gaping eyes.

They rode until midday, when the sun was directly overhead and beating down on the narrow valley, reflecting off the rock walls and the hard scrabble surface and causing distant objects to shimmer. Despite the altitude, and from the labored breathing of the animals Ben knew they were pretty high, the concentrated heat in the valley sucked sweat from their bodies.

There were no trees high enough to provide shade, so they stopped in the first clear area that would accommodate them, and ate. Ben had thought about making a fire, but not knowing what lay ahead of them, decided on cold trail rations. Accustomed to the rigors of the trail, none of the men of the detachment complained, but Heatherton, true to what Ben was beginning to think was his basic nature, lodged a complaint.

"Why can't we make a fire and have a hot meal?" he asked.

"We don't know who took your father," Ben said. "Or how far ahead of us they are. Until I get a better read on the situation, I don't think it's a good idea to light a fire and draw attention."

Heatherton looked around, his eyes widening as if noticing the proximity of the canyon walls for the first time.

"You think someone might ambush us?"

"Let's hope not, but out here, anything's possible."

When they resumed riding, Heatherton rode quietly beside Ben, his gaze darting from side to side, and his shoulders hunched, as if expecting any minute to feel a bullet in his back.

They continued to follow the trail the rest of that day, camped without a fire that night, and resumed following it at first light the next day.

About midday, as Ben was keeping an eye out for an area large enough to stop for a meal, they came around a sharp bend in the narrow canyon they'd been trekking through, and found Hightower stopped, sitting on his horse and looking from side to side, his face wrinkled in puzzlement. Ben looked up and saw that the rock walls to either side curved in toward each other, almost touching at the top, a hundred feet above them. To the front, about fifty yards away, all he could see was a jumble of large rocks and gnarled trees that seemed to be trying to climb up the rocks.

He rode up beside Hightower. "Samuel, have we been following a trail in a box canyon?"

"Sure enough looks like it," Hightower said. "But, that can't be. Ain't no way they could've climbed up these walls."

"Where do the tracks go?"

Hightower pointed down. "From here there ain't

nothin' but rock. No trail to follow. But, 'fore I lost 'em, they was headed straight for that rock wall yonder."

Ben looked down and could see that Hightower was right. The faint tracks that had been visible in the rocky soil disappeared at a surface of cracked shale that spread from one side of the canyon to the other, as if the twelve horses had vanished into thin air.

Ben felt a hollowness in his gut. That many people couldn't just disappear. There had been no side canyons or places to hide even one man.

"They couldn't just vanish," Ben said. He looked at Hightower for confirmation, but the sergeant was staring intently at the tangle of rocks and vegetation in front of them.

"There's got to be a way through that stuff," Hightower said. He turned to Ben, and for the first time since he'd known him, showed emotion. He was confused, and a bit frightened. "That's the only way they could've gone, 'cause horses can't fly."

"So, we'll just have to figure out how they did it." Ben was not about to let the strangeness of the situation get to him. "But, we're gonna have to be careful. If they got some kind of secret passage, it might be guarded."

Hightower nodded. "Or, they could have some kind of traps set. We're gon' have to go slow and careful on this one."

"So, how do you want to do it, Samuel?"

"Mebbe we ought to make camp here, and I'll go on foot and see if I can find the way through."

Ben nodded, turned his horse and started back toward the detachment. Hightower followed. The men, Heatherton included, were staring up at the wall in front of them, and Ben could see varying degrees of worry on their faces.

"Don't fret it," he said, when he reached them. "Looks like the way is blocked. Samuel's gonna scout and see if he can find a way through, but it's gonna take some time, so we'll make camp here. Even if he finds it today, it might be a good idea to wait until morning to go through."

The men began dismounting and grabbing gear, and under Toussaint's command, setting up camp. Ben and Hightower dismounted and walked their horses off a short way, where they tied them to a small tree. Hightower leaned in close to Ben, and in a voice just above a whisper, said, "Another thing, Ben," he said. "I got a feelin' they's somebody on the other side of that wall, or hidin' in all that trash, watchin' us."

Anyone else, and Ben would have asked if he was sure, but this was Hightower, and Ben trusted his instincts. He'd had an itchy feeling for some time himself, and with Hightower's revelation, he realized that was what he'd been feeling. But, who was watching, and from where?

"You think it might be the people we've been following?"

"I don't know, but I'm gon' go find out."

Charles Ray

Chapter 6

While the rest of the detachment busied themselves getting camp set up, Ben approached Heatherton, who stood near his horse looking worried.

"What are we gonna do now, sergeant?" he asked as Ben drew near. "The way is blocked, and we've lost the trail. How can that be?" The words came tumbling out.

Ben took a deep breath. "Sergeant Hightower will find the trail," he said. "He'll also find a way around all that junk up ahead."

His words, for all the reaction from Heatherton, seemed to be falling on deaf ears.

"How in blazes will he find a trail in that." Heatherton pointed. "A tomcat couldn't get through that."

From the external appearance of the jumble of rocks and gnarled trees, the man had a point. But, Ben knew that ten people and twelve animals didn't just disappear into thin air, and if *they* found a way past this little blockade, then Samuel Hightower would too.

"The people we're following got through there somehow," he said. "There was no place they could've turned off, and they didn't double back. If they can get through, I promise you, Sergeant Hightower will too. Now, I recommend you get yourself settled, and get some chow. I think we'll be moving out pretty early in the morning, and it's likely to be pretty rough going from here on out."

Heatherton didn't look convinced, but he nodded and went to join the others. Ben remained where he was, alternating his gaze from the men, busy now around a cook fire, tents already up, and horses tethered, to Hightower, who was changing his cavalry boots for moccasins, as he prepared to scout the invisible trail through the rocks.

After wrapping his boots in a blanket and putting stowing it near the tree where his horse was tied, Hightower gave Ben a look, turned and headed for the wall.

Ben sighed. *Good luck, old friend. Don't let us down.*

Chapter 7

Hightower approached the jumble of rocks, some as large as a pony, and twisted trees. About six feet away, he stopped, and studied the mess before him.

On the surface, the tree limbs were so entwined, and some of the trees appeared to be growing out of the rocks, it looked like the greenhorn Heatherton was right, a cat would have a tight squeeze getting through them. But, he knew well that first appearances could often be deceiving. There was a way through that mess. He just had to find it.

As he did with any job, he stood back at first and tried to get a picture of the whole thing, to get an idea of the amount of work that might be needed in general. What he saw was a tumble of rocks and vegetation about thirty yards wide and fifty feet high, larger at the base than the top. Along with the trees, there were vines of some sort, clinging to rocks and tree trunks near the center of the mass. The overall appearance gave no clue as to how someone could get through the tangles.

He then moved to the left, beginning at the edge of the vegetation, and moved in for a closer look.

He'd made it all the way to the center before he saw

it, then he had to go back for a second look to make sure. At a point about ten feet in on the vegetation, the shine on the leaves didn't look quite right. Upon closer inspection, he noticed that they did not reflect the light quite right, but were dull like the burnished or blued barrel of a rifle, and the green color didn't quite match up with the leaves on the left. He reached into the tangle and rubbed a leaf, feeling the smooth surface between his fingers. Then, he reached to the right and grasped one of the strange looking leaves. It *felt* wrong. He twisted, but there was no give initially. Only after straining until his fingers began to ache was he able to bend the leaf. Well, I'll be dang, he thought, this here leaf's been hammered out in a blacksmith shop and painted green. Inspection of the stems of the vines and the tree limbs revealed that they, too, were painted metal. They had been fashioned by a skilled artisan, and while they wouldn't pass close inspection, from a few feet away, if he hadn't been specifically looking for an opening, Hightower would have taken them for real and moved on.

From that revelation, it didn't take him long to determine the outlines of the gateway; ten feet high and eight feet wide, large enough to accommodate a wagon, it was hinged on the right side, and swung inward easily when he pushed on the left side, revealing a large space between the rock walls some twenty feet high and twenty feet wide, forming a natural tunnel through the mountain. Whoever had constructed this gate was smart, he thought, having it swing inward to keep from scratching the rock surface outside and giving away its location. But for the fact that the tracks he was following had to have gone through this space, he would probably never have noticed it.

He squinted into the gloomy darkness, and in the distance, he could make out a vague arched shape, slightly lighter than the surrounding darkness. That, he thought, must be the other end of the tunnel, but he couldn't even estimate how far away it was. As he peered through the gloom, the feeling of being watched came back, and he heard a scurrying sound like a large rat running across the loose gravel of the tunnel's floor. The darkness pressed down upon him, and he felt a tingling in his back and shoulders as if small insects were crawling over his flesh.

Part of him wanted to turn around and forget he'd ever found this place. But, he could not let Ben down. He took a deep breath and started easing forward, keeping to the center of the space as best he could. The soft soles of his moccasins made whispering sounds on the gravelly surface.

He walked deeper into the tunnel, and for what seemed like hours the light shape at the end seemed to get no closer. But, the scurrying sounds were clearer, and definitely coming from somewhere in front of him. They seemed to be moving away, but it didn't make him feel any better.

Finally, the far end of the tunnel was close enough for him to get a rough estimate of the distance he had remaining to walk, about one hundred yards. Beyond the arched opening he could see gray rocks, brown tree trunks, and dusty green foliage. The indistinct shadows indicated that it was getting late in the day. He breathed out. At least, he wouldn't be venturing into unknown territory in the dark. He kept his right hand near the butt of his revolver anyway. In addition to the smell of dust in the air of the tunnel, he could also smell the musky, dried-grass odor of horse manure, further confirming that riders had passed through. The heavy grassy odor further told him that whoever it was, they'd gone through at least a week or more earlier, which fit with the time Heatherton's father had gone silent.

When he was about six feet from the opening, he stopped. He opened all of his senses in order to get a feel for what lay ahead. He still had the feeling that he was not alone, but he couldn't get a fix on where and who was watching him. He moved toward his right until he came to the wall, and slowly edged toward the opening.

He stopped just inside the arch of rocks and scanned the area outside as far as he could see, and what he could see caused a flicker of emotion. The land beyond the opening was completely different from what he'd just left.

The walls of the mountains rose up higher than he could see from inside the tunnel, but, they appeared to be a mile away, and the land between the opening and the beginning of the slate gray rock was not what he expected. Thick stands of trees grew in among lush green grass right up to the rocks. There were oaks, juniper, and different species of evergreen, and directly in front of the opening, he saw a waterfall cascading down the cliffs and disappearing behind the trees. As he watched, a large bull elk walked out of the tree line and began grazing. To the left, there were waist-high bushes with dark green oval leaves. It was unlike anything he'd ever seen during his entire time in New Mexico Territory, looking more like the area north of New Orleans that he'd visited once right after joining the cavalry more than a decade earlier. The bushes grew right up to the left side of the tunnel opening. Even the soil that he could see just outside the opening was different, dark, almost black, instead of the orangish-brown on the other side.

He moved outside the tunnel and looked around more. Large bushes and trees were on the right. As he scanned that area, the sensation of being watched increased. He kept his head moving, but allowed his gaze to linger on each area of the bushes as he did so. That's when he saw a slight movement of the limbs of a bush, a movement so quick and slight most people would've missed it. He kept his head moving, but was pretty sure that he'd spotted where his watcher was hiding.

Keeping his body alert, he began moving to his left, away from where he'd seen the bushes move, and soon was in the bushes on that side. He kept walking until he was sure he was well into the foliage. Once he felt confident that he couldn't be seen, he crouched down and began working his way back to the edge of the foliage. He made his way to a large bushy plant and squatted on his heels and very, very slowly eased a limb aside just enough to enable him to see the clearing in front of the bush where he'd seen movement.

While he waited, as still as a rock, he kept an eye on the plant. After a few minutes, he saw movement again. He could imagine what must be going through his watcher's mind—he was wondering where Hightower had gone. Well, he thought, we'll just see how long you can wait. As for himself, he knew that he could wait as long as it took.

It took less than thirty minutes. The bush slowly parted, and a figure rose, and after staring long and hard across the clearing, stepped out.

Hightower took a breath, his eyes going wide. His watcher was a boy. In torn blue pants and a black shirt that hung to mid-thigh, he looked to be no more than thirteen or fourteen. Slight of build and no more than five feet in height, with long, scraggly brown hair that reached down to his eyebrows, his face was smudged with dirt. After looking around, he began walking across the clearing. Hightower saw that the toe of his right scuffed brown boot was missing, and the sole of the left flapped loosely as he walked, and pegged him for a runaway living alone here in the wild. That left, though, the question of why he'd been shadowing him near the cleverly concealed gate to the tunnel through the mountain, who had constructed that gate, and why.

The boy drew nearer. Hightower waited, his body coiled like a spring. At the edge of the bushes, not five feet from where Hightower crouched, the boy stopped. Like an animal he sniffed at the air. He cocked his head to the side, listening. Hightower slowed his breathing. With a confused look on his face, the boy finally stepped forward. As he came abreast of Hightower, the sergeant stood.

The boy's eyes went wide. For a moment, he hesitated, as if his mind was refusing to believe what his eyes were telling him. Then, he began turning, but it was already too late. Hightower had stepped forward, his right hand shooting out and grasping the boy's right wrist. The boy opened his mouth to scream. Hightower jerked him in close, spun him and clamped his left hand over his mouth. He made mumbling sounds against Hightower's hand, and writhed in his grip in an attempt to escape.

"Ain't gon' do you no good, boy," Hightower said. "Now, you 'n me, we gon' go talk to Ben 'n you gon' tell me why you out here by yourself, and watchin' me."

Chapter 8

Ben had been watching Hightower inspecting the cliff face. For a moment, his glance moved to the men gathering around the cook fire, and when he looked back, Hightower was gone. It puzzled him, but it didn't worry him over much. Hightower was a capable scout, more than capable than anyone else in the detachment of taking care of himself alone in the wilderness. Looking at the tangled vegetation at the base of the cliff, Ben assumed that his friend had found a way into and behind it, and was exploring, looking for some kind of gap in the rocks that would explain the disappearance of the people they'd been tracking.

The scrape of boots on the hard earth behind him drew his attention. George Toussaint approached.

"Where'd Samuel get off to?" the burly sergeant asked.

"He's out looking for a way through that mountain," Ben replied.

"Well, if there's one to be found, he the one to find it."

"There has to be. That many men and horses don't just disappear." Ben's voice was sharp.

Toussaint took a step backwards.

"Hey, no call a snappin' at me," he said.

"Sorry, George. Guess I'm just wound up about the situation."

Toussaint smiled. "No problem. I been watchin' you 'n that Heatherton fella. He seem to be a burr under your saddle."

"Yeah, for some reason, I just can't warm up to him." Ben scratched his chin. "I'm probably not being fair, though. After all, his pa's missing, and that'd cause anybody to fret. But, he just act so high 'n mighty, it gets to me."

"I know what you mean." Toussaint chuckled. "When I worked the river boats, 'fore I joined the army, they's this one white man what used to ride the boat was like that," he said. "He talk down to everybody, 'n strut 'round like he was the biggest rooster in the hen yard. He seem to have took a special interest in makin' my life miserable, too. Always findin' me, and askin' me to feed his horse, or shine his boots, or somethin'. I swear, I'se at a point, I felt like he say one more thing to me, 'n I'se gon' throw him to the gators."

"What happened?" Ben had heard a lot of Toussaint's stories of what it was like being a black man on a Mississippi River boat filled with gamblers and revelers, but this one was new.

"Well," Toussaint said. "One day, I'se cleanin' the cabin they used for poker, when this young white fella come in and start hasslin' me for no reason. He push me against the wall, 'n I pushed him back. Now, that was a mistake, that could've been fatal for me, if that irritatin' white fella hadn't a been passin' 'long at that moment. That young white fella done pulled this sleeve gun from his coat by then, and was just about to put lead in my hide, when this other fella come in and grab the gun from him. When the young fella start sayin' things like this black boy done put his hand on me, the other fella say he heard the whole thing, and he know the young fella done started it all, 'n if he don't back off and leave me alone, he'd have to deal with him. Well now, that there young fella got all white faced 'n he apologized, 'n when that old man insisted he apologize to me, well, he done just that, and run off. I never seen him again."

Ben made a snorting sound. "That's all well and good, George," he said. "The old man saved your life, but what's that got to do with him irritating you?"

"Well now, I was just gettin' to that part. I swear, Ben, you just about the most impatient person I know. Can't nobody tell you a good story less'n you wants to skip directly to the end." In response to Ben's scowl, Toussaint held h is hands up in mock surrender. "Okay, okay, here's what happen. That old fella say he been givin' me all them odd jobs 'cause he know I wants off of that boat. Did I tell you, he done been givin' me two bits for every job? Well, he did. Ever time he come on the boat, and that was often. I didn't have no place to spend it, so I'd saved up near fifty dollars. Anyway, he say, with that money, I ought to hop off the boat next time it dock in New Orleans, and find me somethin' else to do. And, I plumb did that. Anyways, what I'm sayin' is, sometimes, when a person seem like they bein' unfriendly, it's 'cause they don't know but one way to deal with people, and you have to try to see past the way they act, and try to figure out what they mean."

Ben laughed. "George, you're just about the worst story teller I have ever heard, but your story does make a good point. Thanks."

Toussaint tipped a finger to his right eyebrow. "Glad to be of help. Now, I'm gon' go back and see we get us some supper goin'" He chuckled as he walked away.

Ben watched for a while as Toussaint neared the fire and began talking to Heatherton and the rest of the detachment, as they watched Corporal Marcus

Scott hang a coffee pot on the cross pole above the fire, and then turned back to look at the tangle of foliage and rocks at the base of the cliff. The sun was beginning to get low in the west, and casting long shadows in the valley. It would be dark soon, and he was hoping that Hightower would find a passage through the cliff and get back before too late. After gazing for a long time, he decided that there was nothing he could do about it, so he turned and joined the rest at the fire.

They'd finished their meal of fried beef slices, beans, and hard tack, and were on their second cup of coffee, and Ben had posted guards; Corporal Isaac Harris watching their back trail, and Corporal Hezekiah Layton on the cliff side; while the rest sat around the fire with him. It was full dark, with only the fire casting an orange circle that didn't even illuminate their tents, and Ben was beginning to feel uneasy that Hightower hadn't returned. He could sense the tension in the others as well, Heatherton included. The only sounds were the crackling of the wood burning in the fire and the mournful call of a dove somewhere in the distance.

Heatherton finally broke the silence around the fire. "Why is your man not back yet?" he asked.

"He'll be back, don't worry," Ben said. He tried to sound confident, but in truth, was beginning to worry himself.

"Yo, the camp," a voice called out of the darkness.

Ben let out a breath. It was Hightower's voice.

"It's Sam," Layton said from his sentry point some forty feet distant from them.

"Sam, over here by the fire," Ben called.

When Hightower walked into the circle of illumination from the fire, no one noticed at first that he wasn't alone. The boy, who Hightower held by his upper left arm, cowered behind the sergeant, his eyes darting from one to the other of the dark-skinned men sitting around the fire, and his skinny body, under tattered clothes, shivering like the leaves of a willow tree in a mild wind.

"Who you got there with you?" Toussaint asked.

Hightower pulled the boy forward into the light. "Don't know. He won't tell me his name. Ain't said a word since I grabbed him. By the way, I found a way through that cliff; a gate over a tunnel, and I saw tracks on the other side. Same folks we been trackin'. This here little fella been watchin' us for some time now, too."

Ben rose and stood in front of the cowering boy.

"That true, boy? You been watching us? Who put you up to that?"

His eyes wide with fear, the boy shrank backwards. When he bumped into Hightower, he made a squealing sound and tried to dart away. Hightower clamped hands on his shoulders, and the boy started struggling and making moaning sounds. He struggled so hard, it was hard for Hightower to hang on to him.

"He been doin' that the whole way back through the tunnel," Hightower said. "He actin' like he seen a ghost or something."

Heatherton, who had been sitting beyond Toussaint, stood and walked forward. Upon seeing him, the boy stopped struggling and stared up at him.

"M-mister," he said. "What you d-doin' with the Sons of Ham? You in charge here? C-can you help me, please?"

Heatherton looked puzzled. "What is he talking about, Sergeant Carter?"

At first, Ben, too, was puzzled. Then, he remembered something he'd heard once from an old preacher who'd come through the small town in East Texas where he and his father lived. The wizened old man had given a sermon about the great Flood, and Noah and the Ark, and told of how Noah's sons had treated him. One son, Ham, had laughed at Noah, and in punishment, God had marked Ham with dark skin and cursed his descendants to forever be servants. This, the old preacher had said, was the justification for black people to be held as slaves, the curse of Ham. He wondered where the boy had heard the story.

"He's talking about the fact that we're colored," Ben said. "He must be figuring, because you're white, you must be our owner."

Heatherton's brows arched upwards. "B-but, there's been no slavery now for over ten years, and we never had all that many slaves here in New Mexico. Why would he think that?"

"I don't know, and it hardly matters," Ben said. "What's important is it seems he'll talk to you. Maybe you can find out who he is, and why he was watching us."

"But, in order to do that, I'll have to act like you men are indentured servants. My family never owned slaves, and as far back as I can remember, every Heatherton's been anti-slavery. I just don't know."

Heatherton's expression was plaintive.

"Don't worry," Ben said. "Just get his confidence. Maybe, if you get him to trust you, you can explain things to him. Thing is, he might know who has your father."

Heatherton looked down at the ragged boy, his expression skeptical. He shrugged. "Okay, I'll give it a try." He knelt in front of the boy, who shrank back from him. "Don't worry, son," he said. "I'm not going to hurt you, and neither are any of these men." The boy relaxed slightly, but still looked as if he'd bolt if given the chance. "My name's James Heatherton. Can you tell me your name?"

The boy looked up at him with wide eyes. "M-my name is Moses, sir," he said, his lips trembling. He looked past Heatherton at Ben, who stood quietly behind him. "D-do these men belong to you?"

"Belong to me? Why, no, they don't. Why would you

ask that?"

"You m-mean, they ain't your slaves? How come you be with them, if they don't belong to you?" Moses frowned in puzzlement.

"Slaves?" Heatherton frowned and glanced back up at Ben. "Why would you think they're slaves? These are free men."

Now, Moses puzzled expression deepened, and Ben saw naked fear in his eyes.

"But, we work for him," Ben said.

Heatherton frowned, and opened his mouth to speak, but Ben placed a hand on his shoulder and shook his head slightly.

"What kind of work do they do for you?" the boy asked.

Before Heatherton could respond, Ben said, "We're helping him look for his father. He and some other people were up here in the mountains, and he's afraid they might be in trouble. Have you seen anyone wandering around up here lately?"

Moses blinked, and darted his gaze from Ben to Heatherton. "N-naw, I ain't seen nobody 'cept y'all."

Heatherton's shoulders tensed. Ben squeezed his shoulder lightly. "Uh, Mr. Heatherton, can I talk to you a minute?"

Heatherton stood. He looked down at the boy for a long time before turning to Ben. Ben walked a few feet away, on the other side of the fire, and Heatherton followed.

"What is it, sergeant?" the man asked in a low voice.

"The boy's lying," Ben said. "It could be because he's just nervous with all of us hovering over like we are, I don't know."

"You think he *has* seen my father?"

"I don't know, but he's hiding something. Look, I'm gonna have the men move back into the shadows, and let you talk to him alone. He seems not to be too scared of you."

"You think that'll work?"

"I don't know, but what other choice do we have?"

"I suppose you're right," Heatherton said. "But, I don't have any experience in this kind of thing."

Ben chuckled and patted the man's arm. "I don't either, but he'll talk to you. Just try to put him at ease and see if you can get him to tell you something. For starters, what's a boy his age doing out here all by himself? He's got to have family somewhere. See if you can get him to talk about 'em. I'll be nearby so I can listen if you need help."

Heatherton didn't look confident, but he finally nodded and went back around to the boy. He knelt next to him, but kept an arm's length distance between them.

"Okay, Moses," he said. "Let's start over, okay? Where's your family?"

The boy squinted up at him, his head cocked to one side. He reached up and swiped the hair from in front of his eyes. "They live t'other side of the rocks, back in a little valley."

"Do they know you're out here all alone?"

The boy hesitated. "N-naw, they don't. I was just out doin' a little huntin', and I saw you folks. I was j - just curious is all, so I was watchin' you."

"Can you show us where you live?"

"W-why do you need to see where I live?"

"I just want to see that you get safely home, lad," Heatherton said. "I wouldn't feel right leaving you out here all by yourself."

"T-that's okay. I can get home by myself. You don't need to do that."

"But, I insist." Heatherton looked over his shoulder at Ben, who stood nearby, just outside the circle of illumination from the fire. Ben nodded.

Moses eyes were wide, and his gaze darted from side to side. Watching, Ben could see that the boy was close to panic. He was convinced that he was hiding something, and he could see from the look on Heatherton's face that he was coming to the same conclusion. In fact, Ben thought, the man was doing a good job with the boy. He hadn't gotten any details from him, but he had elicited reactions that told Ben the boy was the key to finding Heatherton's father.

"Well, Moses, what do you say?" Heatherton asked. "We'll take you home in the morning."

With a defeated look on his face, the boy nodded.

"Now," Heatherton continued. "I'll get you a blanket, and some food perhaps, and then you can get some sleep. We'll leave first thing in the morning."

Moses began looking around. At that point, Ben stepped out of the shadows.

"Oh, and Moses," Heatherton said. "Don't try running away. I'll have my . . . men on guard all night. I wouldn't feel right if you went off in the dark and got hurt."

With that, Heatherton stood and turned to face Ben. His left eyebrow lifted, and he had a questioning look in his eyes. Ben smiled and nodded.

Charles Ray

Chapter 9

Ben posted guards in positions so that the boy could see them, and he instructed them to make sure he didn't slip away.

The next morning, he woke up before the sun's first rays showed over the tops of the surrounding cliffs, and the sky was still a dark, pearl gray. Moses Colby lay wrapped in the blanket they'd given him, near the dying embers of the fire, his eyes covered by the hank of dirty brown hair. Ben could tell, though, from the stiffness of the boy's body, that he was only pretending to sleep.

He picked up his canteen and walked over to where the boy lay, and knelt beside him. Moses didn't move.

"I know you're awake," Ben said. "You want a drink of water?"

After a few moments, Moses reached up and brushed the hair from his eyes. He looked up at Ben warily, scrunching back from him. Heatherton, just coming out of the tent Ben had had erected for him, stood and walked over. He took in the scene, and then walked to Ben and reached for the canteen.

"Let me try," he said quietly. He removed the cap from the canteen and took a drink. "See, Moses, it's safe to drink. Sergeant Carter won't hurt you."

He proffered the canteen to the boy. Moses' eyes darted from the canteen to Ben, and back again. Then, he reached up and snatched it from Heatherton's hands, put it to his lips, and throwing his head back, began gulping from it.

"Looks like he was thirsty," Ben said. "I wonder when was the last time he had anything to eat or drink."

Moses lowered the canteen and stared up at Ben. "Yestiddy morning," he said. "When the Prophet left me to keep watch for . . ." and then, realizing that he'd said too much, he snapped his mouth shut.

Ben and Heatherton shared a look. "Say," Ben said. "You must be hungry, then." Ben looked around. The other men were beginning to stir from their tents, and the sentries were moving in closer to the fire. "We'll be fixing breakfast in a bit, and you can eat."

At the mention of eating, Moses licked his lips. He looked up at Heatherton.

"Don't worry, son," Heatherton said. "The food's actually pretty good, and you look like you could use a square meal."

"You want some more water?" Ben asked.

Moses looked at him, and then at the canteen in his hands. Finally, he held it up toward Ben, nodding his head.

Ben took the empty canteen, and walked to the stack of supplies near his tent and retrieved another filled one. When he handed it to Moses, the boy hesitated at first, then reached up and took it.

"T-thank you," he said quietly.

"No need to thank me. Just drink this one a bit slower. You don't want to be getting belly cramps from drinking too fast."

He left the boy with the canteen and motioned Heatherton toward his tent.

"You're pretty good with children," Heatherton said in a quiet voice. "You know, I get the feeling he's never seen colored people before, but has heard some strange stories about them."

"I was thinking the same thing," Ben said. "I'm also

thinking he knows more than he's been telling us. For instance, who is this prophet he mentioned. The way he reacted, I think he wasn't supposed to tell us that."

"My thought exactly. What do we do now?"

Ben scratched his head. "Reckon maybe we should take our time this morning, and try to gain his confidence. Then, around midday, let Hightower lead us through the mountain and see if we can pick up the trail on the other side. In the meantime, maybe you could talk to the boy, see if you can find out who this prophet is."

Heatherton nodded. "I'll do my best."

"For now, though, leave him be and let him get used to being around us."

They looked across the fire at the boy, who had sipped from the canteen, but then was distracted by Corporal Nat Tatum who was arranging a big iron skillet over the fire, balanced on two flat rocks he'd found. He took a tin from the mess pack, opened it and, using a spoon, scooped out a lump of lard, which he put in the skillet. When the lard had melted, Tatum took several strips of beef and laid them out in the bubbling grease. They immediately began to sizzle, and the aroma of meat filled the air. The boy edged closer, his eyes fixed on the meat. He licked his lips. Tatum seemed to be ignoring him, but Ben could see that the corporal was watching the boy out of the corner of his eye, a slight smile on his face. When the boy was about four feet away, Tatum used a fork to lift one of the pieces of meat from the skillet. He held it up and blew on it for a while, then, in a slow motion, and without turning, he held the smoking meat out toward the boy.

"Like to take a little taste? he asked.

Moses shrank back, but when Tatum didn't move any closer, he stopped, his eyes fixed on the brown meat hanging from the fork.

"G'on," Tatum said. "It's still hot, but not so much

it'll burn you. Tell me how it taste."

Moses looked up at the corporal, suspicion on his grimy face, but his gaze kept drifting back to the meat held so close. Slowly, as if it was a snake, he reached out. When Tatum didn't pull it away, he grabbed the end and snatched it off the fork, and crammed the entire six-inch length into his mouth. When he began chewing, his eyes went as round as saucers. He chewed a few times, and then gulped the meat down, and looked back up at Tatum, an expression on his face that Ben had seen on hungry dogs who'd just been fed by a stranger. There was still suspicion and hesitation, but not as much as before. Mostly, what Ben saw was hunger. He licked at the trails of grease that leaked from his mouth.

"Want another one?" Tatum asked.

Moses head bobbed up and down, and when Tatum speared another slice of beef and held it out to him, he took it without hesitation. This time, though, he took his time, biting off small pieces, and chewing on them, a look of satisfaction lighting up his face.

"It taste okay?" Tatum asked.

Moses' head bobbed up and down, and when he finished chewing and swallowing the last bit of the meat, he smiled at Tatum.

"Yeah," he said. "That tasted good. What kinda meat is it?"

"That's beef. We buy it from a rancher over in Texas. He don't sell us his best cows, but they ain't bad."

"What's beef? Moses asked. "And, what's cows?"

Tatum's eyes opened wide. "You don't know what beef is? Ain't you ever seen a cow?"

"I don't think so. Is it like a antelope? It taste a mite like antelope meat, but not as stringy. Or, is it like a horse?"

"They ain't got no cows where you come from, but they got horses? What you folks do for meat?"

"Naw we ain't got no cows, we eat what we hunt in the woods. Mostly antelope and rabbit. In the summer, when the weather gets hot, we sometime catch some of the birds, and when we find their nests early in the season, we eat their eggs. Got some beaver back up in the woods 'n we eat them sometime, but beaver meat don't taste good a'tall. We got horses, but only The Prophet and his archangels are allowed to ride 'em.'"

"Jumpin' Jehoshaphat!" Tatum said. "Ain't never heard tell of no place that don't have a cow or two for milk and meat. What about chickens? You surely got some chickens for eggs and meat."

"We got quail, 'n they give us meat and eggs, The Prophet done figured out how to pen 'em up, and the eggs we don't use for breedin', we eats. Is that like chickens?"

"Well, sure is. When I'se a young 'un, we used to raise quail. But, they eggs is a lot smaller than reg'lar chicken eggs. When they roasted, though, quail make good eatin'. That some place you live in. How long you been there?"

"I was born in Eden," Moses said. "Every body was born in Eden."

Standing nearby, listening, Ben and Heatherton nodded at each other and smiled.

"Well, sergeant," Heatherton said. "I think your corporal just found the key to loosening that young man's tongue."

"I do believe you're right," Ben said.

"You want to try a piece of hard tack?" Tatum asked.

"What's hard tack?" Moses looked puzzled.

"It's a biscuit made with flour, water and salt. It's like chewing on a rock, but if you soften it up with the grease I fry the beef in, it ain't too bad, and the grease give it a little flavor."

He reached into the provision sack and pulled out a round, beige shape. About a half inch thick, it looked like it was made of clay. After dipping it in the skillet and coating it with hot meat drippings, he passed it to Moses. The boy took a tentative bite, and began chewing. His face lit up, and for the first time since his arrival, he smiled.

"Hm, that taste good," he said. "I ain't never had hard tack before. My ma makes bread from ground up crabgrass seeds. She says it's the way the Injuns do it. But, it don't taste like this."

"You think maybe your ma would show me how she make flour from crabgrass?" Tatum asked.

The boy's smile disappeared, and he looked down at the ground. "Uh, maybe," he said. "I don't know, though. The Prophet don't cotton to strangers comin' to Eden, 'specially you . . ." He let the words trail off into silence.

"Aw, don't make no never mind," Tatum said. "We got to keep lookin' for Mr. Heatherton's pa, anyway. Say, they's a stream over yonder by them trees." He pointed. "Whyn't you go wash your face and hands. We gon' be eatin' pretty soon."

Moses looked in the direction that Tatum pointed, and his brow wrinkled.

"That's okay, I'll show you where it is," said Hightower, who had just walked up to the fire.

Moses still looked confused.

Hightower stared at him, and then smiled. "Oh, I see," he said. "You ain't got no soap or towel." He walked quickly to his tent, bent and pulled out his saddle bag. From the bag, he took a brown piece of cloth. "You can use this here for a towel, and share my soap." He handed Moses the cloth, and held up a small, white bar of soap.

Moses took the cloth, and followed Hightower into the bushes, beyond which was a narrow, shallow stream they used for washing, cooking and drinking water.

Ben watched them go, knowing that Hightower

would keep the boy from running away. In fact, Ben was thinking, between Tatum and Hightower, they just might win enough of the boy's confidence to get him to talking sooner than Ben anticipated, which meant they might be able to get back on the trail sooner than planned.

The two of them were back at the fire five minutes later, and Moses looked like a different person. The grime was gone from his face, and his unruly hair, now wet, was plastered to his skull.

Tatum handed the boy a plate piled high with beans, fried beef, and hard tack, along with a tin cup of coffee. He looked around, and saw Hightower sitting with his back against a tree eating.

"You m-mind if I sit near you 'n eat?" Moses asked.

Hightower scooted to his left. "Not 'tall, lad. Pull up a bit of dirt and set yourself down."

Moses sat down with his back to the tree, his shoulder only inches from Hightower. Ben and Heatherton moved to a tree about six feet and sat, careful not to seem to be watching the boy.

Moses and Hightower ate in silence for a few minutes. Finally, Moses broke the silence. "Can I ask you somethin'?"

Hightower took a sip of coffee. "Sure, what you want to know?"

"What's them yella marks on your shirt?" Moses pointed at the chevrons indicating Hightower's rank.

"Oh, that's just showin' that I'm a sergeant."

"What's a sergeant?"

Hightower pulled at the lobe of his left ear. "Man, you don't know much do you? A sergeant's somebody in the army who been in a while and done got promoted from corporal. 'Course, you probably don't know what an army is either, do you?"

"I do too know what an army is," the boy said. "That's a whole bunch of people what go out and fight wars against evil, like a host of angels. 'Course, some armies ain't good, like the legions of Satan."

"Okay, I see you got the idea, sort of." Hightower regarded the boy, his lips pursed. "Anyway, I'm in the army, the United States cavalry, and these three stripes tell folks that I'm a sergeant."

Moses cocked his head to one side and squinted one-eyed at Hightower. "Is the Yew-nighted states cav'ry part of Satan's legions?"

Hightower, just taking another sip of coffee, coughed and spewed coffee. "Wha-, naw, boy! Where in tarnation you get a fool idea like that?"

"The Prophet says that the Sons of Ham are part of Satan's Legion, 'n he say that dark people have the mark of Ham on 'em. 'Course, you ain't really black like the Prophet say, more brown like the trunk of an oak tree."

"Well, it's true, my skin ain't black, but black's what people use to describe my people. Just like they use white to describe folks like you, even though your skin ain't really white. You more pink, 'n sometimes, when you been in the sun a long time, you either red or brown. Oh, and the *United* States cavalry ain't got nothin' to do with the devil. Who is this here fella, the prophet, anyway, been tellin' you all this foolish stuff."

Moses frowned. "The Prophet, his name's Jeremiah, and he's the Father of All."

"Well," Hightower said. "He got it all wrong. I ain't got nothin' to do with Satan, and the cavalry ain't part of no legion of Satan. We's out here to protect settlers from Injun raids 'n stuff like that. Ain't you folks in, what you call that place you come from, Eden, ever heard of us?"

"We don't get visitors from outside the valley, 'cept for the pilgrims—" Moses snapped his mouth shut, and looked down at the scraps of food left on his plate.

"Who the pilgrims?" Hightower asked.

"Nobody. Just some folks what come to Eden long time ago, when I was little, and they didn't stay long,"

Moses said in a rush.

Hightower nodded, but regarded the boy with his eyes half closed. He knew he was lying, and sitting nearby, so did Ben.

Ben posted guards in positions so that the boy could see them, and he instructed them to make sure he didn't slip away.

The next morning, he woke up before the sun's first rays showed over the tops of the surrounding cliffs, and the sky was still a dark, pearl gray. Moses Colby lay wrapped in the blanket they'd given him, near the dying embers of the fire, his eyes covered by the hank of dirty brown hair. Ben could tell, though, from the stiffness of the boy's body, that he was only pretending to sleep.

He picked up his canteen and walked over to where the boy lay, and knelt beside him. Moses didn't move.

"I know you're awake," Ben said. "You want a drink of water?"

After a few moments, Moses reached up and brushed the hair from his eyes. He looked up at Ben warily, scrunching back from him. Heatherton, just coming out of the tent Ben had had erected for him, stood and walked over. He took in the scene, and then walked to Ben and reached for the canteen.

"Let me try," he said quietly. He removed the cap from the canteen and took a drink. "See, Moses, it's safe to drink. Sergeant Carter won't hurt you."

He proffered the canteen to the boy. Moses' eyes darted from the canteen to Ben, and back again. Then, he reached up and snatched it from Heatherton's hands, put it to his lips, and throwing his head back, began gulping from it.

"Looks like he was thirsty," Ben said. "I wonder when was the last time he had anything to eat or drink."

Moses lowered the canteen and stared up at Ben. "Yestiddy morning," he said. "When the Prophet left me to keep watch for . . ." and then, realizing that he'd said too much, he snapped his mouth shut.

Ben and Heatherton shared a look. "Say," Ben said. "You must be hungry, then." Ben looked around. The other men were beginning to stir from their tents, and the sentries were moving in closer to the fire. "We'll be fixing breakfast in a bit, and you can eat."

At the mention of eating, Moses licked his lips. He looked up at Heatherton.

"Don't worry, son," Heatherton said. "The food's actually pretty good, and you look like you could use a square meal."

"You want some more water?" Ben asked.

Moses looked at him, and then at the canteen in his hands. Finally, he held it up toward Ben, nodding his head.

Ben took the empty canteen, and walked to the stack of supplies near his tent and retrieved another filled one. When he handed it to Moses, the boy hesitated at first, then reached up and took it.

"T-thank you," he said quietly.

"No need to thank me. Just drink this one a bit slower. You don't want to be getting belly cramps from drinking too fast."

He left the boy with the canteen and motioned Heatherton toward his tent.

"You're pretty good with children," Heatherton said in a quiet voice. "You know, I get the feeling he's never seen colored people before, but has heard some strange stories about them."

"I was thinking the same thing," Ben said. "I'm also thinking he knows more than he's been telling us. For instance, who is this prophet he mentioned. The way he reacted, I think he wasn't supposed to tell us that."

"My thought exactly. What do we do now?"

Ben scratched his head. "Reckon maybe we should take our time this morning, and try to gain his confidence. Then, around midday, let Hightower lead us through the mountain and see if we can pick up the trail on the other side. In the meantime, maybe you could talk to the boy, see if you can find out who this prophet is."

Heatherton nodded. "I'll do my best."

"For now, though, leave him be and let him get used to being around us."

They looked across the fire at the boy, who had sipped from the canteen, but then was distracted by Corporal Nat Tatum who was arranging a big iron skillet over the fire, balanced on two flat rocks he'd found. He took a tin from the mess pack, opened it and, using a spoon, scooped out a lump of lard, which he put in the skillet. When the lard had melted, Tatum took several strips of beef and laid them out in the bubbling grease. They immediately began to sizzle, and the aroma of meat filled the air. The boy edged closer, his eyes fixed on the meat. He licked his lips. Tatum seemed to be ignoring him, but Ben could see that the corporal was watching the boy out of the corner of his eye, a slight smile on his face. When the boy was about four feet away, Tatum used a fork to lift one of the pieces of meat from the skillet. He held it up and blew on it for a while, then, in a slow motion, and without turning, he held the smoking meat out toward the boy.

"Like to take a little taste? he asked.

Moses shrank back, but when Tatum didn't move any closer, he stopped, his eyes fixed on the brown meat hanging from the fork.

"G'on," Tatum said. "It's still hot, but not so much it'll burn you. Tell me how it taste."

Moses looked up at the corporal, suspicion on his grimy face, but his gaze kept drifting back to the meat held so close. Slowly, as if it was a snake, he reached out. When Tatum didn't pull it away, he grabbed the end and snatched it off the fork, and crammed the entire six-inch length into his mouth. When he began chewing, his eyes went as round as saucers. He chewed a few times, and then gulped the meat down, and looked back up at Tatum, an expression on his face that Ben had seen on hungry dogs who'd just been fed by a stranger. There was still suspicion and hesitation, but not as much as before. Mostly, what Ben saw was hunger. He licked at the trails of grease that leaked from his mouth.

"Want another one?" Tatum asked.

Moses head bobbed up and down, and when Tatum speared another slice of beef and held it out to him, he took it without hesitation. This time, though, he took his time, biting off small pieces, and chewing on them, a look of satisfaction lighting up his face.

"It taste okay?" Tatum asked.

Moses' head bobbed up and down, and when he finished chewing and swallowing the last bit of the meat, he smiled at Tatum.

"Yeah," he said. "That tasted good. What kinda meat is it?"

"That's beef. We buy it from a rancher over in Texas. He don't sell us his best cows, but they ain't bad."

"What's beef? Moses asked. "And, what's cows?"

Tatum's eyes opened wide. "You don't know what beef is? Ain't you ever seen a cow?"

"I don't think so. Is it like a antelope? It taste a mite like antelope meat, but not as stringy. Or, is it like a horse?"

"They ain't got no cows where you come from, but they got horses? What you folks do for meat?"

"Naw we ain't got no cows, we eat what we hunt in the woods. Mostly antelope and rabbit. In the summer, when the weather gets hot, we sometime catch some of the birds, and when we find their nests early in the season, we eat their eggs. Got some beaver back up in the woods 'n we eat them sometime, but beaver meat don't taste good a'tall. We got horses, but only The

Prophet and his archangels are allowed to ride 'em.'"

"Jumpin' Jehoshaphat!" Tatum said. "Ain't never heard tell of no place that don't have a cow or two for milk and meat. What about chickens? You surely got some chickens for eggs and meat."

"We got quail, 'n they give us meat and eggs, The Prophet done figured out how to pen 'em up, and the eggs we don't use for breedin', we eats. Is that like chickens?"

"Well, sure is. When I'se a young 'un, we used to raise quail. But, they eggs is a lot smaller than reg'lar chicken eggs. When they roasted, though, quail make good eatin'. That some place you live in. How long you been there?"

"I was born in Eden," Moses said. "Every body was born in Eden."

Standing nearby, listening, Ben and Heatherton nodded at each other and smiled.

"Well, sergeant," Heatherton said. "I think your corporal just found the key to loosening that young man's tongue."

"I do believe you're right," Ben said.

"You want to try a piece of hard tack?" Tatum asked.

"What's hard tack?" Moses looked puzzled.

"It's a biscuit made with flour, water and salt. It's like chewing on a rock, but if you soften it up with the grease I fry the beef in, it ain't too bad, and the grease give it a little flavor."

He reached into the provision sack and pulled out a round, beige shape. About a half inch thick, it looked like it was made of clay. After dipping it in the skillet and coating it with hot meat drippings, he passed it to Moses. The boy took a tentative bite, and began chewing. His face lit up, and for the first time since his arrival, he smiled.

"Hm, that taste good," he said. "I ain't never had hard tack before. My ma makes bread from ground up crabgrass seeds. She says it's the way the Injuns do it. But, it don't taste like this."

"You think maybe your ma would show me how she make flour from crabgrass?" Tatum asked.

The boy's smile disappeared, and he looked down at the ground. "Uh, maybe," he said. "I don't know, though. The Prophet don't cotton to strangers comin' to Eden, 'specially you . . ." He let the words trail off into silence.

"Aw, don't make no never mind," Tatum said. "We got to keep lookin' for Mr. Heatherton's pa, anyway. Say, they's a stream over yonder by them trees." He pointed. "Whyn't you go wash your face and hands. We gon' be eatin' pretty soon."

Moses looked in the direction that Tatum pointed, and his brow wrinkled.

"That's okay, I'll show you where it is," said Hightower, who had just walked up to the fire.

Moses still looked confused.

Hightower stared at him, and then smiled. "Oh, I see," he said. "You ain't got no soap or towel." He walked quickly to his tent, bent and pulled out his saddle bag. From the bag, he took a brown piece of cloth. "You can use this here for a towel, and share my soap." He handed Moses the cloth, and held up a small, white bar of soap.

Moses took the cloth, and followed Hightower into the bushes, beyond which a narrow, shallow stream they used for washing, cooking and drinking water.

Ben watched them go, knowing that Hightower would keep the boy from running away. In fact, Ben was thinking, between Tatum and Hightower, they just might win enough of the boy's confidence to get him to talking sooner than Ben anticipated, which meant they might be able to get back on the trail sooner than planned.

The two of them were back at the fire five minutes

later, and Moses looked like a different person. The grime was gone from his face, and his unruly hair, now wet, was plastered to his skull.

Tatum handed the boy a plate piled high with beans, fried beef, and hard tack, along with a tin cup of coffee. He looked around, and saw Hightower sitting with his back against a tree eating.

"You m-mind if I sit near you 'n eat?" Moses asked.

Hightower scooted to his left. "Not 'tall, lad. Pull up a bit of dirt and set yourself down."

Moses sat down with his back to the tree, his shoulder only inches from Hightower. Ben and Heatherton moved to a tree about six feet and sat, careful not to seem to be watching the boy.

Moses and Hightower ate in silence for a few minutes. Finally, Moses broke the silence. "Can I ask you somethin'?"

Hightower took a sip of coffee. "Sure, what you want to know?"

"What's them yella marks on your shirt?" Moses pointed at the chevrons indicating Hightower's rank.

"Oh, that's just showin' that I'm a sergeant."

"What's a sergeant?"

Hightower pulled at the lobe of his left ear. "Man, you don't know much do you? A sergeant's somebody in the army who been in a while and done got promoted from corporal. 'Course, you probably don't know what an army is either, do you?"

"I do too know what an army is," the boy said. "That's a whole bunch of people what go out and fight wars against evil, like a host of angels. 'Course, some armies ain't good, like the legions of Satan."

"Okay, I see you got the idea, sort of." Hightower regarded the boy, his lips pursed. "Anyway, I'm in the army, the United States cavalry, and these three stripes tell folks that I'm a sergeant."

Moses cocked his head to one side and squinted one-eyed at Hightower. "Is the Yew-nighted states cav'ry part of Satan's legions?"

Hightower, just taking another sip of coffee, coughed and spewed coffee. "Wha-, naw, boy! Where in tarnation you get a fool idea like that?"

"The Prophet says that the Sons of Ham are part of Satan's Legion, 'n he say that dark people have the mark of Ham on 'em. 'Course, you ain't really black like the Prophet say, more brown like the trunk of an oak tree."

"Well, it's true, my skin ain't black, but black's what people use to describe my people. Just like they use white to describe folks like you, even though your skin ain't really white. You more pink, 'n sometimes, when you been in the sun a long time, you either red or brown. Oh, and the *United* States cavalry ain't got nothin' to do with the devil. Who is this here fella, the prophet, anyway, been tellin' you all this foolish stuff."

Moses frowned. "The Prophet, his name's Jeremiah, and he's the Father of All."

"Well," Hightower said. "He got it all wrong. I ain't got nothin' to do with Satan, and the cavalry ain't part of no legion of Satan. We's out here to protect settlers from Injun raids 'n stuff like that. Ain't you folks in, what you call that place you come from, Eden, ever heard of us?"

"We don't get visitors from outside the valley, 'cept for the pilgrims—" Moses snapped his mouth shut, and looked down at the scraps of food left on his plate.

"Who the pilgrims?" Hightower asked.

"Nobody. Just some folks what come to Eden long time ago, when I was little, and they didn't stay long," Moses said in a rush.

Hightower nodded, but regarded the boy with his eyes half closed. He knew he was lying, and sitting nearby, so did Ben.

Chapter 10

After the meal was finished, Ben ordered the men to strike camp. Moses stood near the dying fire, watching in fascination as the cavalrymen efficiently went about the task of striking and folding tents and other gear, and stowing it on the backs of the pack animals. Now and then, one of the men, usually one of the younger ones like Hezekiah Layton or Malachi Davis, would engage him in conversation. Ben watched as, bit by bit, they made the boy a part of the routine, showing him how to properly fold a tent, or to lash down a rope over supplies on a horse's back.

He seemed particularly taken with their weapons; the 1873 Springfield Trapdoor .45 caliber carbines, and the .45 caliber Smith and Wesson Schofield revolvers. He clapped gleefully when Corporal Marcus Scott demonstrated his ability to reload the top break revolver, one-handed and with his eyes closed, in less than thirty seconds. The Prophet, he said when Davis showed him how to load the carbine, only allowed his archangels to have rifles and pistols, mostly old single shot rifles. When asked how they killed game, then, he said that the women and young boys, who did the hunting and food gathering, used snares and pit traps, or knives, and he showed him the six-inch blade knife he had under his shirt.

With the camp struck, and noon still more than four hours away, Ben could see no reason to delay longer. He approached Moses, who stood transfixed watching Corporal Charles Barkley throw his nine-inch blade knife at the piece of cloth tied to a knot on a tree some twenty feet away. Each time the blade pierced the cloth, which was each time Barkley threw it, Moses clapped.

He was clapping when Ben stepped up next to him. He stopped, his hands mere inches apart, and glanced up apprehensively at Ben.

"He's pretty good with that pig sticker, ain't he?" Ben said.

Moses squinted up at Ben for a long time, then smiled. "He sure is," he said. "I ain't never seen nobody could throw a knife like that."

"Say, I reckon you'd like to go home, wouldn't you?"

"Uh, yeah, I would."

"Okay, today, we'll take you home."

Moses' eyes widened. "Uh, that ain't such a good idea. Prophet Jeremiah don't like strangers comin' to Eden."

"I'm pretty sure he won't mind that we brought you home," Ben said. "I can't just leave a youngster like you wandering around here all alone."

Moses closed his eyes. When he opened them, Ben saw a look of cunning on his young face that gave him chills.

"Okay," Moses said. "I'll show you the way to Eden."

After getting the pack animals ready, Ben organized the detachment in two columns and, with Hightower leading, with Moses sitting in front of him, headed for the gateway Hightower had discovered.

The cunning look on Moses' face changed to slight alarm when he saw how easily Hightower opened the gate. Hightower waited until Ben entered and explained how to close the gate, then turned his horse and headed toward the exit at the other end.

Ben was amazed at the size of the tunnel. Even riding two abreast, the walls to either side were obscured in the gloom once the gate was closed, and while he could sense the rocks over them, they were too high to see details. He breathed a sigh of relief when they finally emerged from the darkness, but his eyes went wide at the vista that lay before them.

"I've never seen anyplace like this anywhere else in the territory," he said to Heatherton, who still rode beside him.

"My father told me once that he suspected there were places like this in some of the mountains," Heatherton said. "Enclosed on all sides by the mountains, the winds are blocked and these little valleys have their own weather systems. It probably never snows here, and he said there's probably animals here that exist nowhere else in New Mexico. He has this crazy theory that the Anasazi moved into a place like this, which is why they disappeared."

"Your father seems to know a lot about the territory."

Heatherton frowned. "Yes, if only he spent as much time and energy on the business. These past few years, he's been obsessed with proving his theory, and I've had to take over running the mines, or we would've been out of business already."

Ben sensed that Heatherton wasn't as disappointed at that state of affairs as he claimed, but said nothing.

"You think he found that gate, and has gone in here to explore?"

"It's possible," Heatherton said. "But, it's not like him not to let me know where he's going. I have a bad feeling about this."

"Yeah, me too. Well, let's get this boy back to his folks, and see if we can find where your pa went." Ben turned to the waiting Hightower. "Okay, Moses, tell Samuel which way to your home."

Moses ducked his head, avoiding eye contact with Ben. "Okay." He pointed east. "Eden's over that way, through the opening in them trees."

"How far is it?" Hightower asked.

"Walkin', it takes three days. I don't know how long it takes ridin'."

Hightower began walking his horse east, with the column strung out behind him.

They stopped once at midday and had cold rations, and quickly resumed riding. Moses periodically pointed in a new direction, taking them on a winding course through the towering trees. Around the middle of the afternoon, Hightower pulled his horse to a halt, and looked around, his brown brow wrinkled. He frowned as he looked down at the top of Moses' head, then tapped the boy's shoulder.

"Hang on a minute, Moses," he said, and dismounted. "I need to talk to Ben 'bout something."

Without waiting for Moses to reply, Hightower walked back to Ben and Heatherton.

"What's the matter, Sam?" Ben asked.

"This danged boy been takin' us 'round in circles for the last few hours."

"How do you know that?" Heatherton asked.

Hightower scowled up at the man.

"Trust me, he knows," Ben said quickly. "I saw a look in that boy's eyes back on the other side of the mountain. I can't say I'm surprised."

Heatherton looked frustrated. "So, what are we going to do?"

"Let's stop here and make camp," Ben said. "I'll see if I can talk some sense into him."

Ben signaled for dismount, and the men began setting up camp, as Hightower walked back to his horse.

"Why we stoppin'?" Moses asked.

"We stoppin' 'cause the sergeant in charge say we stoppin', now get off my horse."

His eyes wide, and never taking his startled gaze off Hightower, Moses slipped to the ground.

"What's the matter? You act like you mad at me."

"I am mad at you," Hightower said. "I get mad at anybody who lie to me."

"B-but—"

Hightower made a chopping motion with his hand, cutting Moses off. "Don't make it worse by tellin' another lie. Look, boy, you been takin' us 'round in circles, 'n pretendin' like you was takin' us to your home. Now, you get over there by where they's buildin' the fire, and don't say nothin' more to me."

Charles Ray

Chapter 11

The tents were set up, a fire was going, and a pot of coffee was brewing, within minutes. Moses sat cross legged between Scott and Layton, his shoulders sagging and his gaze on the ground at his feet. Except for Corporals Reuben Kincaid and Isaac Harris, who had been assigned first watch sentry duty, the rest of the detachment and Heatherton sat in a circle around the fire. Scott had mess duty, and was arranging items from the mess haversack in preparation for cooking supper. All eyes were on the tiny figure dwarfed between the two cavalrymen, and the harshest gaze of all came from Hightower, who sat across the fire directly from him, but Moses refused to make eye contact with him.

Ben sat next to Hightower. He could sense his friend's anger. He was, himself, a bit put out by the boy's actions. But, he knew that the situation called for delicate handling—up to a point.

"Now, Moses," he said in a quiet, even voice. "Why were you giving us the wrong directions? Don't you want to go home?"

Moses lifted his head, but had a hard time maintaining eye contact. "Yeah, I want to go home, but . . . it ain't that easy."

"Why is it not easy? Surely, your parents want you home."

"You d-don't understand. Prophet Jeremiah, he don't like strangers comin' to Eden. The only ones he let stay are the pilgrims he chooses."

There was that word again, Ben thought. "When was the last time he chose pilgrims, Moses?"

"About a mo-. A long time ago. I don't remember exactly."

"How many of them did he choose?"

"Four . . . I think."

"Was one of them an old man?"

"I don't know. Maybe."

"Was one a woman?" Heatherton asked.

Moses looked at him quickly, and then away. "Uh . . . no, all four were men, old men."

Ben knew from the way he blinked as he spoke that he was lying. He sensed that pressing him on it, though, wouldn't work, so he changed the subject.

"So, why won't this Jeremiah like us bringing you home?"

Moses licked his lips. He tried meeting Ben's gaze, but failed, and looked down at his feet.

"Come on, son," Heatherton said. "The sergeant asked a valid question. Why don't you answer him?"

He shot Heatherton a pleading look, meeting a stony gaze. Finally, he looked at Ben. "The Prophet says that people with the Mark of Ham, dark skins, come from the devil. He say they ain't like the rest of us, and we have to stay away from 'em."

Heatherton shook his head. "Son, you been with us a couple of days now. Do *you* believe Sergeant Carter and his men are evil?"

Moses' brow wrinkled. He looked from Heatherton to Ben, and then looked around at the other men sitting around him.

"I . . . I don't know. I mean, you done treated me okay 'n all. You seem like good enough people. B-but, ever since I can remember Prophet Jeremiah been tellin' me that people like you come from the devil." His eyes glistened. "Maybe you ain't really got the Mark of Ham. The Prophet said that when Ham laughed at his father, Noah, when he was drunk and naked, the Lord turned him and all his descendants black. But, you ain't really black. You all different colors of brown, 'n you ain't got horns and forked tails."

"It's like I told you," Hightower said. "People call folks like us black. That's mebbe 'cause some of us can be dark enough to almost be black. They call folks like you and Mr. Heatherton white, but you ain't really white, and they call the Indians red, but ain't none of them got red skin. I don't know why, other than maybe it's just a lazy way to describe people. What I *can* tell you is that we ain't part of no army of Satan—there ain't no such thing."

"B-but, the Prophet Jeremiah says—"

"The prophet might be wrong, son," Heatherton said.

Moses' face hardened. "The Prophet is never wrong."

"And, how do you know that?"

"W-well, he says so." Moses dropped his gaze, and his cheeks turned red. "And, my ma say I should always listen to what he say."

"What about your pa?" Ben asked. "What does he say?"

"I ain't got no pa. Prophet Jeremiah is the father of all."

Ben frowned at the boy. He was clearly confused, and Ben doubted that pushing him further for information would help.

"Look, Moses," Ben said. "Why don't you let us take you home. We can explain to . . . Jeremiah that we found you wandering alone out here. He surely ought to be thankful we didn't leave you to be eaten by wolves." As he spoke, Ben wondered about that. The boy had been left to watch them, so this Jeremiah obviously wasn't worried about him. He wondered, though, about the boy's mother. How could a mother allow her child to be left alone like this?

"I don't know," Moses said. "The Prophet ain't likely to change his mind about strangers. If you was pilgrims, he might let you stay, but . . . I don't think he'll accept anybody but Mr. Heatherton here."

"We're willing to take that chance." Ben's voice was firm. "Tell you what, you sleep on it. We'll talk about it again in the morning."

Chapter 12

The next morning, after breakfast, Ben had them strike the camp. He approached Moses, who lingered by the dying fire, staring at the smoldering embers.

"You ready to go home?"

Moses turned and looked up at Ben, his eyes shining with unshed tears.

"I can't do it. I'm sorry, but I just can't."

"Why not? Don't you want to go home?"

The boy blinked. A thin line of water leaked from his left eye. He wiped at it with his hand and looked plaintively up at Ben.

"You don't understand," he said. "Whyn't you just leave me be. I can find my own way home." He stood abruptly, pushed past Ben and ran into the bushes behind the camp site, where he leaned against a tree, his body shaking.

"Something's really eating at him," said Heatherton, who had come up near the end of the conversation.

"He's scared of something," Ben said. "And, I don't think it's us."

Heatherton clasped his left hand over his right fist, holding them near his chest. "Yes, I noticed that. Especially when he talks about this Prophet Jeremiah and his archangels."

"Something's going on in this place called Eden." Ben rubbed his chin. "And, I have a feeling that's also where we'll find your father and his crew."

"What makes you say that?"

"Things he's said, and the way he's said them," Ben replied. "He's mentioned pilgrims a few times, and then caught himself. When he said the last ones came a long time ago, and they were all old men, the way his eyes kept shifting tells me he was lying."

"So, you think my father's in this Eden place?"

Ben sighed and shrugged. "I can't tell you why I do, but yes, I think your father and the others are in Eden, and I don't think they're there of their own free will."

Heatherton seemed to shrink; his shoulder slumped, and his face went slack. "And, the only person who can tell us where this Eden is, won't. What do we do, sergeant?"

"I'm just gonna have to think of a way to get that boy to tell us. Let me think on it. I'll come up with something."

With a dejected look on his face, Heatherton walked away. Ben stood alone. As was often the case since he was given command of this special detachment of soldiers, it was left to him to find a way to accomplish a seemingly impossible mission. His main mission was to find Heatherton's father and his group, but in order to do that, he would have to break through the fear the boy, Moses, seemed to have of this Prophet Jeremiah, and the conditioning he'd obviously experienced for a long time, probably his whole life from the way he talked.

He waited, and watched the boy until he seemed to relax a bit, then he walked over.

"You feeling better, Moses?" he asked.

"Yeah, I guess."

"You mind if I ask you a few questions? You don't have to answer any that you don't want to, okay?"

"Okay."

Ben moved to the tree, on the opposite side from Moses.

"Were you born in Eden?"

"Yeah."

"You have any brothers or sisters?"

"Everybody in Eden's brother and sister. That's the way the Prophet Jeremiah runs things."

"What's your ma's name?"

"Sarah, my ma's name is Sarah."

"And, your pa?"

"Jeremiah is my father."

It wasn't lost on Ben that Moses used the term 'ma' for his mother, and 'father' for the Prophet.

"I don't mean the prophet, I mean your ma's husband," Ben said.

"I know what you mean. The Prophet *is* my father. He's husband to every woman that lives in Eden."

It took a few seconds for what the boy said to sink in. Ben felt as if a cold wind blew across his body. The only people he'd ever heard of who practiced such marital customs were the Mormons, and most of them lived in Utah Territory, having been so persecuted back east, they'd packed and left in order to be able to continue to follow their customs.

"You people in Eden Mormon?" he asked.

"What's a Mormon?"

Dang, Ben thought. This gets stranger every time this boy opens his mouth.

"How many women live in Eden, Moses? How many wives does this Jeremiah have?"

The boy closed his eyes and, rubbing his right thumb and forefinger began counting silently. When he opened his eyes, he said, "There's thirty women in Eden. Then, there's another twenty-five girls and eighteen boys. 'Bout fifteen of the girls soon be able to become mothers."

Ben stared at the boy, hardly able to believe what he was hearing. "So, what will your prophet do when they do? Since he fathered them, he can't . . . he wouldn't—"

"No, The Prophet wouldn't do anything like that,"

Moses said. "He'll give one girl to each of his ten archangels. The rest'll go to the pilgrims. That way, we get new blood in Eden, 'n we won't die out, accordin' to The Prophet."

Keeping his expression neutral, Ben leaned around the tree. Moses was loosening up, and had just about confirmed that this Jeremiah had the elder Heatherton, and he didn't want to spook him until he knew more.

"What about the boys?" he asked. "Won't be long until you'll be old enough to be thinkin' about gettin' married. Where you gonna find a wife, if everyone is Eden is brother and sister?"

"One of the older boys will marry the woman pilgrim, and The Prophet—" Suddenly, Moses stopped talking and clapped a hand over his mouth. "Uh, The Prophet says he'll see to us when the time comes."

Ben had heard almost enough. The pilgrims *had* to be Heatherton's crew, which had consisted of three men and, Cady Logan, a twenty-eight-year-old who worked as a part-time housekeeper for William Heatherton, according to his son, and who also had an interest in the old man's studies, accompanying him and the others on their expeditions. Now, all he had to do was convince Moses to show them the way to Eden.

"You know, Moses," Ben said. "It'd be a lot easier if you'd just show us how to get to Eden. Then, we could take you home."

Moses made direct eye contact with Ben for the first time, and when he spoke, for the first time, Ben thought he was telling the absolute truth.

"I'm sorry, but I can't do that," he said. "Prophet Jeremiah taught me that all dark people were part of Satan's army, but now that I got to know you, I ain't so sure about that. Now, if he's wrong about that, what else is he wrong about? I don't know. What I do know is that if you go to Eden, he will kill you."

Ben patted the revolver at his hip. "We know how to

take care of ourselves, Moses."

The boy's eyes glistened as his gaze bore into Ben. "But, he wouldn't just kill you. He done said many times that it's better to die than be a part of the world of Satan. He'd kill me, my ma, and everybody else in Eden, too."

Charles Ray

Chapter 13

For several seconds, Ben stood, his hands on the tree trunk, his mind reeling. There was no doubt in his mind that Moses had meant it when he said that Jeremiah was prepared to sacrifice every resident of Eden rather than submit to any outside authority. The man was mad, and he'd taken Heatherton's father and his people—for what purpose Ben could only speculate, but from what Moses had said, it wasn't good.

The setup in Eden, from Moses' sketchy description, reminded Ben of the Ku Klux Klan, an organization formed in Tennessee in 1865, after the War of Southern Insurrection and the start of Reconstruction, by a group of disgruntled white men, aimed at protecting southern whites from northern abolitionists and the newly freed blacks. The KKK, as it came to be known, specialized, though, in intimidation of blacks and their white supporters, with bands of hooded men staging night raids, and committing acts of violence aimed at instilling fear. They had not been into withdrawing from society, and threatening suicide. Their aims were to reestablish their dominance over the newly-freed population of former slaves. The organization had been disbanded in 1870, when the government in Washington withdrew federal troops from the south and effectively ended reconstruction, but remnants of the hate they'd spread remained, with small bands of robe-wearing, hooded hooligans cropping up from time to time to sow fear in black communities. Jeremiah's group, though, was another breed entirely, and the implications gave him chills. His mission was to rescue Heatherton and his people, a job that would be difficult enough against a Klan-line group, but against people who would willingly die, it seemed impossible.

He leaned against the tree, a morose expression on his face. The sound of footsteps on the hard ground caused him to push away from the tree and turn.

Hightower, his own expression grave, stood there, his campaign hat in his hand.

"Looks like you didn't get much out of the boy," he said.

"Yes and no," Ben replied. He then told Hightower what Moses had told him.

"Dang, that means he ain't gon' tell us how to find Eden."

"Yeah, and from what he told me, I don't think we got time to traipse over these mountains looking for them."

Hightower scratched his head and then settled his hat on it. "Mebbe we can get him to *show* us where Eden is," he said.

"How do we do that?"

Moving in close and leaning over so that his mouth was only inches from Ben's ear, Hightower said. "If we look the other way long enough, that boy's gon' rabbit, 'n head for home. When he do that, I can trail him 'n find out where it is."

Ben smiled. The simplest way to deal with the issue, and he hadn't thought of it. Of course, the boy would run away at the first opportunity, and he'd head for home. Hightower, who could move through the forest as silently as a shadow, would have no problem following him without him being aware of it.

"That, Samuel, is a good idea. Find out from George who's on sentry duty tonight, and make sure they know not to pay too much attention to the camp. We'll see what happens."

"He's gon' rabbit, you just watch."

Charles Ray

Chapter 14

And, rabbit he did.

After supper, Layton gave Moses a blanket, which he rolled himself in and lay down near the fire. Hall and Kincaid had sentry duty, and posted themselves about twenty yards from the cluster of tents, with their backs to the fire. Hightower, explaining that he preferred being able to see the stars as he fell asleep, lay wrapped in a blanket near the tent he normally shared with Toussaint. He lay on his back, with his eyes closed, but cracked the lids just enough to be able to see the sleeping form near the fire. Ben was in his own tent, but had the flaps open, and from inside, like Hightower, he lay with his eyes open, and in a position that allowed him to see Moses at the fire.

From where he lay, Hightower could clearly see the rhythmic rise and fall of the blanket draped over the boy. Beyond him, the outline of Lucas Hall, his back to the boy, was but a barely discernible bit of darkness against the trees and cliffs beyond. He slowed his breathing and relaxed his limbs the way he'd been taught by Squamo-tok, his foster father. Anyone observing him, lying there on his side, his eyes half open, might have assumed he was one of those rare persons who sleep with eyes open, or even mistaken him for a dead man, so still was his body. But he was neither asleep, nor dead. His eyes, ears, and nose took in everything with perfect clarity; the shape of the boy wrapped in his blanket, outlined by the flickering flames of the fire, the soft cooing of a mourning dove in the distance, and the odor of pine wood burning in the fire; all were present, and he noted all, discarding those of no consequence, and focusing on those that were important.

As a consequence, when the body beneath the blanket stiffened, Hightower noticed. He watched as Moses slowly and carefully pushed the blanket aside. After a few moments, the boy sat up slowly, and looked around. When there was no other movement, Moses came to his knees and, grabbing a couple of the loose limbs piled near the fire, wrapped them in the blanket and spread it out in a loose approximation of a sleeping figure. Then, after looking around again, he stood and moved slowly toward his right, aiming at a point some ten feet to the right of Hall, who sat with his head down and his shoulders slumped, as if he'd fallen asleep at his guard post. Once past Hall, Moses began walking faster, until he was swallowed up by the bushes. Only then did Hightower move.

As quietly as Moses had, he slipped from beneath his blanket, and began moving in the same direction the boy had gone, his moccasin-clad feet making only the faintest of whispering sounds. As he passed Hall, the latter turned his head and smiled, his face just visible in the dim glow from the fire. Hightower nodded and slipped into the bushes where he'd seen Moses disappear.

He was only a few seconds behind him, and despite Moses' efforts to move quietly, Hightower's sharp hearing picked up the brushing sound of the boy's body moving through the thick foliage. His own passage, though, was even more silent than that of a gentle breeze. From the sound, he estimated that Moses was only ten feet or so ahead of him; close enough that he could continue to track him through the bush in the dark from the sounds he made, but not so close that Moses would hear him.

The trek through the bushes lasted for thirty minutes, with the boy following a relatively straight course toward the northwest. Hightower knew when he left the bush when the rustling sound of his passage abruptly stopped. He picked up his own pace, and soon was at the edge of the thick bushes himself.

About fifteen feet away, easy to see in the light from the full moon that hung high in the sky, the slight figure of Moses moved quickly over a broad plain that seemed to stretch onward into infinity to the north and west, bounded on the east side by a dark line that was the bushes and trees through which they had just traveled.

Hightower waited until Moses was a good twenty feet away before stepping out of the darkness of the bushes and settling in behind to follow him. The boy moved much faster now, his course directly north, toward a dark forest that grew up the lower parts of the towering cliffs for about a hundred feet. Above that level, the rest of the cliffs jutted upward, gray against the blackness of the night sky, forming a wall that encircled them.

They walked for over a mile across the plain, Hightower marveling at how distance was distorted in this . . . valley surrounded on all sides by high mountains. From time to time, Hightower would move off to the side ten or fifteen feet, just in case Moses looked back, but, once the boy left the bushes, he kept his head forward, walking fast, almost running, and heading for a break in the trees. From the determined way he walked, Hightower guessed that Eden was not far away.

The tree line toward which Moses walked turned out to be farther away than Hightower had estimated. The sky in the east was already beginning to lighten by the time the boy arrived at the break in the trees, and walked between two towering trees. After a few paces, he began walking down, disappearing from view from the ankles up. Hightower rushed forward, darting to the side and into the tree line.

He made his way to the side, keeping low behind bushes, until he could peer through the leaves and see over the little spine of earth that Moses had disappeared behind.

A clearing lay below, roughly circular, and ringed by juniper and pine trees, in which were fifteen small log cabins. Smoke rose from the chimneys of all but one, a cabin at the far side of the clearing, where two men armed with rifles stood to either side of the door. To the left of this cabin was a stable, in which twelve to fifteen horses milled around, snorting and making whinnying noises.

He saw Moses approach the nearest cabin. "Ma, I'm home," the boy called in a hushed voice, as he rapped softly on the door.

The door opened, and a woman walked out. She looked mouth agape at him. Moses ran forward, and the woman embraced him.

"Moses, my baby, you finally come home," Hightower heard the woman say. "The Prophet said he left you to watch in case anybody came lookin' for the pilgrims. I reckon nobody did, right?"

Moses hesitated, before saying, "Naw, ma, nobody came, and pretty soon I run out of food. I got tired of eatin' nuts and berries, so I come back home.

"Well, we better wake The Prophet up and let him know."

"Do we have to, ma? I'm powerful hungry. Couldn't I eat something first?"

"We can't do that, Moses," she said, her voice quivering. "You know how The Prophet is. We go tell him, 'n then I'll fix you a big breakfast. But, we got to tell him, first."

A tall man, dressed all in black, with long, white hair, and a white beard that covered most of his face, came around the corner of the building.

"What is it you have to tell me, Sarah? Ah, Moses, you have returned. Did anyone come looking for the pilgrims?"

Moses stepped away from the woman and turned to face the old man, his shoulders slumped and looking at his feet.

"N-no, Prophet," he said. "I waited for a l-long time, until my food run out, and nobody come, nobody at all. So, I come back to tell you."

The man walked to Moses, reached out and caught his chin, lifting the boy's head and glared down into his eyes.

"You absolutely sure, boy? Nobody came looking?"

"Y-yes, sir. I done stayed in the bush near the camp site, just like you told me, 'n nobody come, not nobody at all."

The man released Moses' chin, and after another moment of staring, patted his shoulder. "Okay, Moses, you did good, real good," he said. "Now, Sarah, you give this boy something to eat. I reckon with nothing but nuts and berries for the past few days, he's powerful hungry."

The woman, Sarah, and Moses both bowed toward the man, who regarded them down the length of a long, straight nose.

"Thank you, Prophet," Sarah said. "I'll do that."

The man patted Moses' shoulder once more. "After you eat, get yourself some rest, boy. We're having a community meeting come noon, and I want you rested for it."

From where he crouched in the bushes, Hightower couldn't see the expressions on their faces clearly, but the way they cringed in front of the old man, he thought they were scared.

He took one last look at the entire area, committing the layout to memory, and then eased back in the bushes. After a few feet, he stood, and began trotting.

.

Chapter 15

After watching Hightower disappear into the darkness on the boy's trail, Ben lay back on his blanket, but he was still unable to sleep. His mind was in turmoil as he wondered what his friend would find out there in this unknown wilderness.

At some point he drifted off to sleep, tossing and turning under his blanket, and finally, when the first rays of sunlight from behind the towering cliffs began to turn the sky a dull gray laced with stripes of orange, his eyes popped open.

He pushed the blanket aside, sat up and stretched to ease the kinks from sleeping on the hard ground. Yawning, he looked out toward the fire. Toussaint knelt by the fire, adjusting the coffee pot over the flames. After a minute, the odor of coffee drifted across and tickled his nose. As much as he wanted a hot cup of coffee, though, the pressure on his bladder took precedence.

After slipping on his boots, he grabbed his haversack, rose and made his way to the area, downslope a bit from the tents, where they'd set up a latrine. He relieved himself, then went to the stream, upstream from the latrine, and performed his morning toilet routine; splashing his face with the chilly water, brushing his teeth, and then, using a straight razor and a bar of lye soap, hacking at the stubble that had grown on face overnight, only nicking himself once shaving with cold water—something he hated, despite having done it for over a decade.

With his haversack stowed back in his tent, he joined Toussaint at the fire. The burly sergeant handed him a cup of coffee. He held the steaming liquid under his nose for a few minutes, breathing in the aroma, and letting the warmth of the cup restore circulation to his fingers. Only when he felt the tingle from renewed blood flow to his fingertips, did he take a sip of the almost scalding brown liquid.

After the hot liquid had slid down his throat, warming him inside all the way to his stomach, he sat back on his heels and sighed.

"You don't look like you got much sleep last night," Toussaint said.

Ben looked across the fire at Toussaint's bloodshot eyes. "You don't look all that good yourself."

Toussaint blew on his own coffee, and then took a sip. "Naw, I tossed 'n turned all night," he said. "Guess I'se worried 'bout Sam. He oughta be back by now."

Ben wanted to say that he wasn't worried, that Hightower knew his way around the woods, and would be okay, but the truth was, he was also concerned. He didn't know what was out there, and while he was not one to shy away from battle, the unknown gave him pause. Still, he couldn't let his worry affect his men.

"He'll be okay. If there's anybody who can make his way through this wilderness, it's Samuel."

He knew from the way Toussaint regarded him with narrowed eyes over the rim of his cup that he wasn't convinced. But, he just nodded, and sipped his coffee.

"So, we just gon' stay here and wait for him?"

"Not much else we can do. Who's got mess duty this morning?"

"Marcus," Toussaint said. "He had first watch last night, though, so I thought I'd let him get a few extra minutes sleep this mornin'. Since we ain't goin' nowhere, it won't hurt if breakfast's a little late."

"I'm done sleepin'," a sleepy-sounding Scott said,

emerging from his tent, yawning, stretching, and talking all at the same time. "You two's makin' so much noise, a body can't sleep no way."

Ben chuckled as the corporal, fully dressed except for his boots, which he was hopping around putting on, glared in their direction. After adjusting his boots, Scott pulled his haversack from the tent and stood. "I'm gon' get cleaned up, 'n then I'll get chow started." He went off toward the latrine.

"Should I rouse the rest of the detachment?" Toussaint asked.

Under ordinary circumstances, Ben would've had the entire detachment up and busy by now, but since they would likely be camped in the same place for at least the rest of the day, and he had no idea what lay ahead for them, he decided to let the men get as much rest as possible.

"No, wait until Marcus gets back and gets breakfast started," he said.

So, the two of them sat back and enjoyed their coffee. When Scott returned, stowed his haversack, and began preparing the morning meal, Toussaint put his cup away and went to wake the detachment. Soon after, the camp site was abuzz with activity, as men washed, shaved, and got ready for the day. They cheered when Ben said there would be nothing to do after breakfast, except for posting two sentries.

With that business out of the way, he tried to enjoy his food, but his mind kept wandering to Hightower.

It was about noon, and Ben felt like saddling his horse and heading off to try and find Hightower's trail, when he looked up and saw the sergeant emerge from a clump of brush to the north of the camp site.

Hightower walked with purpose, but without rushing, and when he approached Ben, standing near the fire, his expression was impassive.

"It's about time you got back, Samuel," Ben said. "I was beginning to worry." He said the latter in a low voice that only Hightower could hear, which still earned him a scowl.

"Didn't see no need to rush," Hightower said. "Eden ain't goin' no place."

"You found it?"

"That boy led me straight to it."

"Did you see any sign of Mr. Heatherton's father or the others?"

"Well, I didn't *see* 'em, but I'm pretty sure they got 'em. There was one cabin with guards."

"Is it far from here?"

"It's 'bout a three-hour walk, so on horseback, I'd say 'bout an hour."

"Then, we head out right after we eat."

Hightower smiled, a slight lifting of the corners of his mouth. "That's good, 'cause I'm hungry enough to eat my saddle. That jerky I took with me just ain't fillin' enough. Feels like my stomach's got a fight goin' with my belt buckle."

Chapter 16

After eating their midday meal, Hightower cleared a space near the cook fire, and began briefing Ben and the detachment on Eden.

He started by drawing squares to represent the cabins as best as he recalled them, including a larger square to represent the stable.

"These are the cabins," he said. He pointed to one in the rear, that sat apart from the others. "This one here had two guards at the door." Then, he pointed to one at the very front. "And, the boy, Moses', ma 'n him live in this one."

"How many people there?" Toussaint asked.

"I didn't stay too long. I just saw the old man with a beard; this Jeremiah fella; Moses, his ma, the two men with rifles, and the stable. 'Course, it was early in the mornin', and I reckon most folk was still asleep."

"Did you see a way to get to that guarded hut without being seen?" Ben asked.

Hightower shook his head. "Naw. From the front, you have to pass a whole bunch of cabins, and from the back, it's a long stretch of clear ground. Plus, you'd have to get around the side, and it'd be hard to do that without bein' seen."

Ben stared down at the drawing, trying to think of an appropriate next move. If they'd known for certain that those they sought were being held in the settlement, it would be a different matter—perhaps, but without that knowledge, he was severely constrained in his actions. He couldn't very well ride in and accuse Jeremiah and his flock of kidnapping. If wrong, it could create a large problem for the Ninth, whose men were only grudgingly accepted by many of the white residents of the territory, and then mostly when they were in need of cavalry assistance. Laying false charges against a group of people wouldn't improve their standing at all. On the other hand, he thought, even if he *knew* that this Jeremiah held Heatherton's father hostage, he couldn't just ride in, guns blazing and rescue them. The settlement contained women and children, and in the absence of information to the contrary, he had to assume that they were innocent. It would *really* hurt the cavalry's image if they got caught in a crossfire. Despite all these impediments, though, he would somehow have to accomplish his mission.

He looked across the fire at James Heatherton, who stared down at Hightower's drawing, his expression somber. During the course of the mission, Ben's impression of the man had undergone a change. In fact, the man's behavior had changed. He no longer acted superior to the cavalrymen, and often pitched in to help set up and break camp. He'd even volunteered to take a turn at mess duty and stand sentry.

Ben now realized that his initial brusqueness had been due to his worry about his father's fate. Realizing that the soldiers shared his concerns had rubbed the rough edges off his personality.

Ben felt that he owed it to him to rescue his father, a personal obligation, and he never shirked from personal obligations.

"Anybody got any ideas?" he asked.

Corporal Charles Barkley leaned forward and raised a finger. "How 'bout we send a couple of people 'round to get in behind 'em, and the rest of us ride in the front. Then, we ask 'em if they got the hostage, and demand they turn 'em over."

Just like him, Ben thought. A frontal charge, with minimal back up, and no reserve. A fearless warrior, Barkley was always the first to pull the trigger whenever Ben gave the order to open fire, and the last to stop shooting. This situation, though, called for a little more finesse.

"The problem with that," he said. "Is, if they do have 'em, they're likely to start shooting, and some of the women and children in that settlement could get hurt, 'n if they don't have 'em, we could be stirring up a ruckus for no reason."

"We could scout around and keep a lookout on the place," Hightower said. "See if we can spot the hostages, 'n then mebbe come up with a plan to rescue 'em."

Ben nodded, and smiled at him. "That's not a bad idea. I suppose there's lots of places we can spy from?"

"Oh, yeah. There's thick brush in front, and it's kinda on a ridge, so you lookin' down at the settlement. There's a pretty worn trail leadin' in from the front, but looks like the bush is solid in back."

"So, one way in and out?"

Hightower's head bobbed up and down. "Yeah," he said. "Sorta got 'em trapped, but it also means any mounted attack gets funneled on the trail. Ain't gon' be easy to sneak in."

Ben stood and brushed at his trouser legs. "Okay, let's go take a look at Eden."

Charles Ray

Chapter 17

Striking camp and riding to a point about a quarter mile from the ridge marking the entrance to Eden took them three hours. It was late afternoon, so Ben decided they would find a suitable camping site deep in the trees to avoid someone from Eden accidentally stumbling across them, and they would wait until morning to begin scouting the place.

The site he chose was a small clearing, about thirty yards off the path, and not far from a shallow stream. He decided against setting up tents, just in case they had to leave quickly, and also that there would be no fire. Even if the fire wasn't seen, the smell of wood burning would carry far in the thin air, and give their presence away. That, of course, meant they'd be eating cold rations again, but it was something the men of the detachment were accustomed to. Ben expected to hear complaints from Heatherton, but the man cheerfully accepted his hardtack and jerky, and washed it down with water from his canteen.

Ben assigned Hall and Kincaid first watch, and ordered everyone else to get as much sleep as possible. He, himself, slept fitfully, waking up in time to make sure the second watch was up and at their posts, and then finally waking up before the sun rose.

After getting cleaned up, and washing down jerky and hardtack with water, he woke the men, and allowed them time to wash and eat.

Sitting in a circle, all eyes were on Ben.

"Okay, here's what we're gonna do," Ben said. "George, Samuel, and Mr. Heatherton will come with me. We're going on foot to get a close look at the settlement. The rest of you wait here, and stay out of sight. Once I've seen what we have to deal with, we'll make a plan."

"Why am I going?" Heatherton asked.

"I'll explain when we get there," Ben replied curtly. "Okay, let's move."

He stood and turned away from the frowning, confused looking civilian and stepped up beside Hightower. Hightower nodded and headed off in the direction of the settlement, with Ben and the other two men close behind.

After a ten-minute walk, Hightower dropped to one knee, and motioned them to do the same. Carefully, he parted the foliage, allowing them to see the little bowl-shaped valley just below them.

It was much as he'd described it, a middling-sized community of log cabins, with three rows of four each in the front, each with a small garden at the side, a slightly larger cabin centered behind them, and two more rows of cabins behind that. To the left, and set back ten yards, was a large, wood rail fence corral, with a small log hut to its left, with twelve horses milling around inside the corral, and off to the right, a small, windowless log hut, with a single door. Two men, dressed in black and holding long rifles across their chests, flanked the door. Several people, mostly women draped in gray muslin one-piece dresses, or children; boys in brown trousers and gray shirts, girls in dresses like the women; were engaged in a variety of activities. Some of the women worked in a large plowed field off to the right, while others were tending fires near the cabins, or washing clothes in a stream that ran from north to south behind the corral. A tall man, dressed in black, with long white hair and a white beard covering much of his face, stood in front of the largest cabin, deep in conversation with six black-clad men, all armed with rifles. With the exception of the guarded cabin and the small hut near the corral, each cabin had a stone chimney from which white smoke drifted upward. From where they crouched, watching, other than the armed men, it looked much like any peaceful frontier settlement.

After an animated conversation, which they couldn't hear, the bearded man waved his arm, and one of the armed men gave his rifle to another and started toward the front cabins.

"Looks to be about thirty people," Hightower said. "And, just the nine men have weapons."

"Yeah," Ben said. He turned to Heatherton. "Any of those men look familiar to you?"

Heatherton squinted through the gap in the foliage. "No, but look at that corral." He pointed. "See that roan horse with the white blaze on its forehead? That's my father's horse. I'd recognize it anywhere, even from this far away."

Ben shifted his attention to the corral. The roan stood out in a herd of mostly gray or black horses, and one pinto.

"You sure that's your pa's horse?"

"No doubt. See that dark spot on its left hindquarters, just in front of the tail? How many horses you think there'd be with the exact same coloration? No, that's my father's horse, all right."

That cinched it for Ben, at least as far as whether or not the people they'd come to rescue were in the settlement. Now, he just had to come up with a plan to rescue them.

"Okay, then," he said. "I imagine they have 'em in that cabin with the guards. Problem's gonna be getting *to* that cabin past all the others . . . in other words, the entire settlement."

"I see nine men," Heatherton said. "Surely you soldiers can handle that number, can't you?"

Ben had no doubts about the outcome of a gun battle between his seasoned troopers and the nine men with their old fashioned looking long rifles, but that wasn't his first choice of a plan.

"We probably could," he said. "But, there's women and children down there, and I don't like risking their lives in a gunfight. Besides, we don't know where they're holding the hostages, or even if they *have* them for sure. We need to think of a way to rescue them without shooting, if possible."

Heatherton looked skeptical, and a bit angry. Ben could understand that, and sympathize to a point. If he thought *his* father was being held hostage by these people, he'd likely be thinking the same thing. But, he was in command, and, while his job was to rescue the hostages, at the same time, as a soldier in the United States army, it was his job to protect the innocent, and unarmed women and children, even if they were part of the community that had taken the hostages, were not to be harmed. He scanned the scene below, looking for anything that might offer him an answer to the puzzle he faced. Heatherton, though, was not done.

"So, we're just going to sit here and do nothing?"

"No," Ben said. "We're not. George, go back and get the detachment. Leave one man with the horses, and bring the rest. We'll set up an assault position here, while I try to come up with a plan."

Toussaint nodded and faded back through the bushes. Ben, Hightower, and Heatherton settled on their haunches to wait.

He still hadn't come up with anything when Toussaint returned with seven troopers, carbines across their chests, following him.

"I left Reuben guarding the horses," he said as he knelt next to Ben. "What you plannin' to do?"

"I don't rightly know, George. We're only guessin' that the hostages are in that guarded cabin at the rear, and with all the women and children down there, if we go in showin' our weapons, a lot of them could get hurt."

Toussaint squinted down at the settlement. "Well, we could wait 'till dark, and mebbe sneak down to that cabin 'n surprise the guards."

"I thought about that," Ben said, shaking his head. "But, if we get spotted, there'd still be shootin', and in the dark, some of the innocents would be sure to be hurt. Can't take that chance."

"So, what we gon' do, then?"

"I'm thinking on it, George." Ben felt frustration welling up, and knew that his tone had been shorter than he'd intended. *Dang, no sense taking it out on the men.* "Sorry, I haven't come up with a good idea yet. Let's move back a bit, and maybe the two of us can come up with something that has a chance of working."

Toussaint smiled and nodded. Just as they were moving away from the line of bushes through which they'd been observing the settlement, a commotion below drew their attention.

A man in black exited the cabin on the right in the first row. He was dragging a struggling Moses by the arm, and behind them, Sarah, his mother, walked, her arms outstretched, and a look of terror on her face.

"No, you can't do this. You can't take my baby," she said, her voice rising with each word.

"The Prophet said to bring the boy," the man said. "You don't dispute the word of The Prophet, Sarah."

"B-but, Moses didn't do nothin' wrong."

"Now, that's for The Prophet to decide, ain't it." The man jerked the boy, who was half his height and less than half his weight, so hard, his heels dragged across the ground. "The Prophet will judge whether he's guilty or not."

"But, what is he guilty of?" The woman shrieked and pulled at her hair.

"Just you come along, Sarah, 'n The Prophet will

tell you."

The man dragged the boy around the side of the cabin and toward the white-bearded man and the others, who stood waiting in front of the larger cabin. Wringing her hands and crying, the woman followed.

"That don't look good," Toussaint said.

"No, it doesn't," Ben said, nodding in agreement. "Somehow, they must know the boy saw us and didn't tell 'em. I have a feeling that this *prophet's* judgement won't be merciful."

They watched as the women and children who were working outside were motioned by one of the armed men to assemble in the clearing around the larger cabin, and another went around knocking on doors rousing those still inside. Within minutes, a large crowd of docile, cowed-looking people, dressed mostly in gray, with the six men in block interspersed among them, gathered in front of the large cabin. In front of them, standing in front of the cabin's door, were the bearded man, with a slump-shouldered Moses next to him.

"What we gon' do?" Toussaint asked.

How in blazes am I supposed to know? Ben felt like screaming, but he clamped his lips tight for a moment to gather his thoughts. In every mission, it came down to this, that moment when he, the commander, had to make a decision one way or another.

"We got to find out what's going on over at that cabin," he said. "And, we're not gonna do that from here."

Toussaint's brows rose and his eyes went wide. "Ben, you ain't sayin' what I think you sayin', is you?"

Chapter 18

"It's the best way to do it without risking a lot of lives," Ben said.

"Yeah, but these folks is crazy, Ben," Toussaint said. "You heard that boy, Moses; that Jeremiah fella don't like colored folk. You go walkin' in there with your dark skin, and they gon' fill you full of holes."

Ben knew that that *was* a possibility, but was hanging his hope on the fact that most people don't just start shooting unless they're immediately threatened—he hoped.

"That could happen, but I don't think it will. If I can get him talking, maybe we can get this settled without anybody getting hurt." He put a hand on Toussaint's shoulder and squeezed. "And, just in case I'm wrong, and I don't make it, you're in charge, George. You do what you have to do." Looking at the serious look in his friend's eyes, he didn't have to ask what Toussaint would do. Ben handed him his carbine.

"You goin' in there without your weapon?"

Ben patted the revolver at his waist. "I don't want to get them excited. Besides, I'll have this. If they decide to shoot me, having that ain't gonna make much difference."

"Okay, if you just gon' have to be mule-headed about this," Toussaint said.

Heatherton, who had stood by watching and listening to their conversation with his mouth agape, proffered a hand to Ben.

"Sergeant Carter," he said. "You are an exceptionally brave man. I do hope that your plan works."

"So do I," said Ben. "Now, you go on with George, and just in case the shooting starts, keep your head down."

Heatherton smiled, and turned to follow Toussaint. Ben stood there, watching them walk away. When they were out of sight, he turned back toward the settlement, squared his shoulders, and started walking down the slope toward the cabins.

He encountered no one as he passed one, then another line of cabins, getting to where he could hear conversations ahead, when he arrived at the third row. With one more row of cabins between him and the crowd, he stopped and peered around the corner of the second cabin from the left in the third row.

While all of the other cabins had small gardens behind or to the side, the area around the big cabin was clear, hard-packed earth, which was now covered by the residents of the settlement, all facing the bearded man, who stood in front of the door of the cabin, a gnarled hand on young Moses' shoulder.

"People of Eden," the bearded man said in a deep voice that sounded to Ben like the old itinerant preachers he remembered hearing as a child. "The boy Moses has been examined, and found guilty of betraying the community."

"No," a woman's voice wailed. "Not my baby, not my Moses." Ben recognized the voice of Sarah, the boy's mother. "Jeremiah, you can't do this."

The bearded man, Jeremiah, scowled at her and pointed.

"That's *Prophet* Jeremiah to you, Sister Sarah," he said. "You are coming dangerously close to heresy, you know."

The woman fell to her knees, her arms outstretched.

"Forgive me, Prophet," she said. "I meant no disrespect. But, I know my boy ain't never betrayed us."

Jeremiah pushed Moses toward one of the armed men, who grabbed the boy's arm. He then strode over to Sarah, still on her knees.

"Sister Sarah," he said with menace in his voice. "Are you questioning me?"

"N-no, Prophet, I would n-never do that. B-but, I know my son, and I know he would never betray you or the community."

"And, *I* say that he has betrayed us." He stood, arms folded across his chest, and faced the crowd. "The boy's got the smell of wood smoke in his clothes. He was left to watch and see if anyone came looking for the pilgrims . . . he was left without matches or a way to start a fire. In fact, he was told *not* to start a fire. The only way he could get the smell of smoke in his clothes is if he sat by a fire."

"B-but, Prophet," Sarah said. "It gets c-cold in the mountains at night. Maybe he built a fire to stay warm."

Turning, he pointed his finger at her. "Then, he disobeyed a direct order," he thundered. "And, that's about as bad as betrayal. I told this boy not to build a fire. If he disobeyed me, *that* is disloyalty, and for that he must be punished."

Sarah pitched forward, her forehead in the dirt. "Please, don't punish him," she said in a muffled voice. "Take me instead."

"No, Sarah," Jeremiah said. "For all your willfulness, you are still one of my favorites. I will not have your body marked." He pointed toward the man holding Moses. "Tie the boy to the pole. Administer fifty lashes. The community will observe." His voice rose, almost to a shriek. "Let everyone see the price of disobedience."

The man holding Moses leaned and picked up a

whip from the base of the cabin. Eight feet long, with a two-foot long piece of wood wrapped in leather, and six feet of braided leather in a single tail, ending in a little tuft, the whip was similar to ones Ben remembered seeing some of the slave overseers carry when he was smaller, just before he and his family were emancipated. Since, he'd seen similar devices used by the Texas cowboys in dealing with the longhorn cattle. In the hand of even a neophyte, a bull whip could flay the skin off a person's back. The boy, Ben knew, would not survive fifty lashes.

He could not allow it.

Ben stepped forward between the cabins, coming to a stop just past the fourth row, and about six feet behind the back of the crowd.

"It's not the boy's fault," he said. "He didn't do anything wrong."

Chapter 19

At first, no one reacted to Ben's presence.

Then, one of the women at the back of the crowd turned, and, upon seeing him, put a hand to her mouth and let out a loud shriek.

The piercing sound of her scream galvanized the crowd, starting with those closest to Ben and quickly communicating itself to the front.

Keeping his hands out from his sides, and away from the revolver at his waist, Ben stepped forward. Women and children shrank away from him as he neared them, the women grabbing the younger children and shielding their eyes.

One of the armed men stepped forward and began raising his rifle. Ben's right hand dropped toward the butt of his revolver.

"Stop," Jeremiah shouted. "He might not be alone. We need information first."

The man froze in place, his rifle still pointing at the ground. Ben's hand hovered inches from his weapon.

"I'm not here to hurt anyone," Ben said.

Jeremiah stepped through the crowd until he faced Ben from about ten feet away. "Why are you here . . . boy?"

Ben stiffened, but kept his face impassive. He hoped that Toussaint had had time to get the detachment into positions.

"You have four people here against their will," he said. "I'm here to take them home."

Several of the people closest to Ben gasped audibly. Jeremiah blinked, and then his eyes narrowed to slits.

"No one is in Eden against their will," he said.

Ben looked around. From the way the women cowered whenever Jeremiah spoke, or whenever one of the armed men neared them, he doubted the man's words, and from the way the man had reacted and responded, he was sure that the hostages were indeed being held.

"I don't believe you, sir," Ben said. "In fact, I believe you're holding the hostages in that cabin way in the back."

Jeremiah took an involuntary step back. His eyes blazed, and he turned to look at Moses, who backed up against the cabin wall, tears streaming down his face.

"Did you tell him that, boy?" Jeremiah thundered.

"No, he didn't," Ben said before Moses could respond. "Me and my men have been watching this settlement for a while, and since that's the only place with guards on it, we figured that's where you must be holding hostages or prisoners. Then, of course, there's Mr. Heatherton's horse in your corral."

He'd stressed the 'we' so that Jeremiah and his men would think twice before doing something stupid, but it was the mention of Heatherton's name that got a reaction from the bearded man.

"How do you know his name?" he asked.

"Because, his son came to us for help."

While Jeremiah hadn't reacted to Ben's words, the armed man nearest him began looking nervously up at the ridge line. He moved closer to Ben.

"How many up there?" he asked.

"Enough to lay waste to this place. You know how big a cavalry troop is?"

"N-naw, but I reckon it's a buncha men, right?"

Ben nodded. "More 'n you got here, and everyone of 'em is battle-hardened. We been fighting Indians and outlaws here in New Mexico Territory for a whole lot of years."

He folded his hands across his chest and stared at Jeremiah.

Jeremiah stared back. He stroked his beard, his head cocked to one side.

"Now, look here . . . sergeant . . . there ain't no need for violence. We here in Eden just want to be left alone. That's why we come here in the first place. Now, you wrong 'bout us having this, what'd you say his name was, this Heatherton fella, so why don't you just go on back where you come from, and we ain't gonna have no trouble."

"I'm afraid it's not that simple, mister. I *know* you're holding the people I'm looking for, and I'm pretty sure it's against their will. So, I can't leave without 'em. There's also the fifty lashes you're planning to give the boy. He's done nothing wrong. My scout spotted him the other side of the tunnel through the mountain before he saw us, and we followed him. That's not his fault. I got one of the best scouts in the territory. He was raised by Indians, and can track better than an Indian. So, I can't let you punish the boy for what's not his fault."

"What we do here in Eden ain't none of the army's business," Jeremiah said.

"But, it *is* our business. One of our jobs out here is to protect people, and if you whip that boy with a bull whip fifty lashes, it'll kill him, and I can't let you do that."

Jeremiah stepped forward until he was standing close enough to Ben to reach out and touch him. Behind the bushy beard and mustache, his chapped lips were curled up into a half-smile.

"You're an interesting specimen, sergeant. What's your name?"

"Benjamin Carter. First Sergeant Benjamin Carter, Ninth U.S. Cavalry."

Stroking his beard, Jeremiah began walking around Ben, looking at him the way ranchers looked at a horse they were considering buying. It made him uncomfortable, and a bit angry, but Ben remained still, his gaze on Moses, who still cowered against the cabin wall.

After making the circuit, Jeremiah, once again in front of Ben, folded his arms across his chest.

"I never knew many of your kind, Sergeant Carter," he said. "Except for a few of the slaves on the plantations near where I grew up, and, of course, I never had any truck with them. I'd heard when the War of Northern Aggression started, that the northerners were recruiting colored men to fight, but I never thought that experiment would work out. Everybody knows that you colored don't make good soldiers."

"There were a lot of your Johnny Rebs thought that until the first time they came up against a colored regiment in battle," Ben said. "So, they had plantations where you come from. They've never had plantations here in New Mexico, so where was your home before you came here?"

"I lived in a little town called Mission, in Texas, south of the Red River, not far from where Louisiana, Texas, and Arkansas come together. It was just me 'n my ma and pa on a little dirt farm, but there were some cotton and sugar cane plantations nearby."

Ben was familiar with the area; just north of where he grew up. Many of the soldiers who joined the southern brigades came from there, and at war's end, when they returned, they brought with them a sense of lawlessness and violence that turned much of the eastern strip of Texas, as far south as Houston, into a kind of no-man's land of violent little towns and squatter camps, where liquor was cheap and life was cheaper.

"So," Ben asked. "How'd you come to be this far

west?"

"Things in Mission get bad when the war started," Jeremiah said. "With most of the able-bodied men off fighting, there wasn't anybody left to supervise the slaves properly. My pa was sickly, so when the Confederates come through recruitin' men, they passed me by so I could stay and take care of my ma." He tugged at his beard. "When that ape, Lincoln, freed the slaves in 1962, it got really bad. A lot of the slaves up and run away to the north, 'n some others decided to take land they said was owed 'em. Pretty soon, it was evident that them northern devils was gonna win, 'n was likely to set the colored against us, so in 1863, me 'n a few more of the men that was left in Mission, gathered up a few women 'n wagons and headed west. We figured the war hadn't hit way out here as bad, 'n we'd find a place to settle where we wouldn't be bothered."

Ben kept his expression neutral as he shifted his gaze from Jeremiah and let it drift slowly over the armed men mixed in with the crowd, paying special attention to the one nearest him, who kept looking warily at him, but kept his rifle pointed at the ground.

"We're not here to bother you," Ben said. "But, if you have Mr. Heatherton and his people here, I need to be able to make sure they're here of their own free will."

The small amount of flesh on Jeremiah's cheeks that Ben could see above the wild tangle of white hair flamed red, and the chapped lips quivered.

"You accusin' me of forcin' people to stay here? We don't need to force people." He waved his arms jerkily. "Just ask any of 'em if they want to leave. You have my permission."

Ben looked at the fearful faces of the women and the confused looks on the faces of the younger children. He was pretty sure of the answers they'd give with Jeremiah's armed men standing guard. But, as much as he sympathized with them, they were not his immediate problem.

"How about you let me talk to Mr. Heatherton," he said. "If he tells me that he and his people want to stay, my men and I will go back to Fort Union."

"We don't have anybody named Heatherton here," Jeremiah said.

"Now, Mr. Jeremiah, I'm not one to call a man a liar, but when I mentioned him before, the way you talked to Moses there, makes me think he *is* here, and I'm pretty sure that roan with the blaze on its face is his horse."

The red on Jeremiah's face now contrasted sharply with the white of his beard.

"For one who don't want to call a man a liar, you just called me one, sergeant. Where I come from, that'd be cause to call a man out as a matter of honor. But, a white man and a colored man dueling . . . well, that just ain't done, so what are we gonna do with you."

"I say we teach this boy some manners, Prophet," the man near Ben said. "I'd be happy to do it for you."

Ben turned to face the man. "If I were you, mister, I'd make sure I kept that rifle pointed at the ground. My men are crack shots, and the minute you raise that rifle, one of 'em's gonna put a bullet through your head."

The man frowned, and a flicker of fear crossed his face as his glance slid from Ben to the distant line of bushes.

"I think you just bluffin'," he said.

"Do you really think I'd come out here alone?"

"He has a point Aaron," Jeremiah said. "Soldiers always travel in groups. I reckon when he says he got sharpshooters drawin' a bead on us, he ain't bluffin'. I tell you what sergeant. Whyn't you just go on back where you come from, 'n we'll just pretend you was never here."

"I can't do that. I need to talk to Mr. Heatherton . . .

and, I can't let you kill the boy."

Jeremiah raised his hand, pointing a bony finger at Ben. "What happens with my son ain't your concern, now, less'n you want to take the punishment in his place, I suggest you be on your way."

Ben wasn't about to turn and walk away. In the first place, he didn't trust Jeremiah and his men enough to turn his back on them, secondly, he wasn't leaving without Heatherton and his group, and finally, he couldn't stand by and allow Moses to be killed by this mad man. His options, though, were few. He wanted to avoid a gun fight.

"I can't do that," he said. "But, I don't believe it's right for the boy to be punishcd unless he's had a proper trial."

"He has been examined by me, and found guilty," Jeremiah said. "That's all the trial he needs."

"Now, you strike me as an honorable man," Ben said. "Somebody who knows the way the law works. When you examined Moses, did he have somebody who could speak for him?"

Jeremiah looked confused. "I am the final judge of right and wrong in Eden."

"But, whether you like it or not, Eden is part of New Mexico Territory, and the United States. Before you can punish a person, they need to have their say, and since Moses is just a child, he ought to have somebody speak for him. Did he have that?"

"There ain't nobody here who knows the law well enough," Jeremiah said. "I'm the only person here who can read or write."

Ben saw a chance. It was a long shot, and it might fail, but it also might delay things long enough for Toussaint to figure out a way to do something that didn't involve a gun battle.

"No, there is one other person here who can read and write, and who knows a little about the law," he said.

Jeremiah looked around. No one in the crowd, including the armed men, would meet his gaze. "Who is that, pray tell?"

"Me," Ben said. "I'll represent Moses, and we can have a proper trial."

Chapter 20

At first, Jeremiah was wide-eyed, and then, he laughed. The way he laughed, high pitched like the yowl of a hyena, gave Ben chills. The man was truly mad.

"You, a colored man, think you know enough law to go up against me?"

"I think I do."

"My, my, things have changed out there since we left. Wasn't too many colored folks who could even read or write when we moved out here. It was against the law to teach 'em."

Ben nodded. "Yes, things have changed. So, you agree to a trial?"

"Okay, you want a trial, we'll have a trial," Jeremiah said. "We'll even have a jury, if you want."

"I think that would be fair."

"I will, of course, be the judge. I'll also be the prosecutor."

"It's not usually done that way."

"Look around. Other than you 'n me, you see anybody else here who could do it?"

"Okay, I see your point."

"Oh, and I have one other condition."

"What's that?"

"If you prevail, and the boy's found not guilty, he won't be punished. If, on the other hand, you lose . . . you share his punishment." He smiled, a small stream of spittle dribbling from the side of his mouth.

Charles Ray

"Guess I don't have much choice, do I?" *George, I hope you get here and get here soon.*

Chapter 21

It took a few minutes for arrangements to be made, and for Jeremiah's court to be set up.

Two of the men moved a hand-crafted wooden table and chair from Jeremiah's cabin and set it up just in front of the door. Jeremiah put a worn, leather-bound copy of the Bible in the center of the table. A woman brought a smaller version of Jeremiah's table and two chairs from a nearby cabin and set it up in front of and centered on Jeremiah's table. The bearded old man walked through the crowd, tapping women on the shoulder until he'd selected six, who were told that they would serve as jury to determine Ben and Moses' fates. They went to their houses and retrieved chairs, which they arranged in a row, to the side of and perpendicular to the big table. Two men, with rifles across their chests, stood flanking Jeremiah, while the rest of the men, minus the two who still stood guard in front of the rear cabin, stood behind the rest of the settlement's women and children, who stood behind the table where Ben and Moses sat.

Ben looked at the jury, but none of them would make eye contact with him, instead, keeping their gazes down at their feet. So much for an impartial jury, he thought. Jeremiah had so much sway over these women, it would take a miracle to get them to come to any decision but the one he told them to come to. Next to him, Moses sat with his shoulders slumped and shivering. *I know how you feel, boy. I'm scared, too.*

He reached over and laid a hand on the boy's shoulder.

"Don't you worry none, Moses," he said. "Everything's gonna be okay."

Moses looked up at him, his eyes glistening.

"No, it ain't. The Prophet's done already decided I got to be punished. Now, you're gonna get punished too. Why'd you come here, anyway?"

"I have a job to do. I have to try and rescue Mr. Heatherton and his people."

"But, why you tryin' to help me?"

"I don't know if I can explain it to you, Moses," Ben said. "But, our job out here is to protect people. I couldn't just walk away and let you be beaten to death. Hell fire, boy, I couldn't do that even if it wasn't my job."

Moses' lips quivered, and then the ends turned up, just a small amount, but Ben knew he was smiling.

"I think The Prophet been teachin' me wrong. You just as good as any man I ever known, better'n any I know, in fact."

"That's the way. This ain't over yet."

Ben patted his shoulder.

"This court is now in session," Jeremiah said in a voice that echoed off the cabin walls.

Chapter 22

No one had to say, 'quiet in the court,' or call for order. All eyes were on Jeremiah as he stroked his beard and looked around the clearing. Finally, his gaze stopped on the six jurors, who were still studying their feet intently.

"Ladies of the jury," he said. "We are hear today to determine the innocence or *guilt* of our brother, Moses, who is accused of betraying the community, and of the interloper, Sergeant Carter, who has come uninvited to Eden and interposed himself in our lives." He then swung his head until his gaze bored into Ben. "How do the two defendants plead?"

"Not guilty, both of us," Ben said.

"Let the boy speak for himself."

Moses looked up at Ben, who nodded, and then turned and looked at Jeremiah. "N-not g-guilty," he said.

"Good lad," Ben whispered.

"Very well, we shall proceed," said Jeremiah. "We're goin' to show that the accused, Moses, son of Sarah, did, with malice in his heart, and with complete disregard for the sanctity of his community, did lead strangers into that community, and not just any strangers, but one who bears the mark of Ham." He laid his left hand on the Bible and rested his right hand atop the left, and, with his head tilted back, stared down his nose at Ben. "Do you have an opening statement?"

Ben stood. "I do. "I maintain that Moses here is innocent of the charges you put against him. He did not lead me to this community willingly. In fact, I followed him here, along with my men, and he was unaware that he was being followed."

"We only have your word on that." Jeremiah pointed a finger at Ben. "Why should we believe you?"

"What reason do I have to lie? If the boy had willingly led us here, why did we not come with him, instead of waiting almost two days?"

Jeremiah blinked. It was a quick movement, but Ben noticed. A flicker of uncertainty.

"Furthermore," Ben pressed on. "We mean no harm to your community. If we'd meant to harm you, I wouldn't have walked in here alone."

He saw two of the six jurors, heads still bowed, sneaking a look at him. Moses' mother, Sarah, standing in the front of the group behind Ben, stepped forward. "What he says makes sense, Prophet," she said. "He could have killed us, and taken what he wants, but—"

"That'll be all from you, Sister Sarah," Jeremiah shouted. "There will be no more outbursts from the audience. The only people allowed to speak are me and the sergeant."

Over his shoulder, Ben saw her shrink back into the crowd, but not before she gave him an imploring look. He turned back to Jeremiah.

"She's right, you know," he said. "I could have taken this place easily. But, I'd rather settle things peaceably. You let me talk to Mr. Heatherton and his people, and promise not to punish Moses, and this can all be over."

"It will be over when I say it's over." Jeremiah glared at him.

"Yeah, that seems to be the way things work here in Edan," Ben said. "You tell what people what to think, right. It's always what you want, never what anybody else wants."

Jeremiah stood and glared across the table, fire in his eyes, his body tense. He raised a hand, finger pointing at Ben.

"*I* am the appointed one," he said in a thunderous voice. "I have been chosen by God to lead this flock into the wilderness, away from the place of iniquity and depravity. I lay down the law as given to me through the Word." He stabbed a finger at the Bible on the table.

Ben realized that the man was close to losing it. He needed to regain the initiative, but he was dealing with someone who knew a lot about religion and the Bible, and was probably expert in interpreting that book in any way that suited him. Ben's own knowledge was limited to what he could remember from the itinerant preachers, when he and his father would go to the Sunday services, every Sunday when his mother was alive, but less and less after she died, until they finally stopped going altogether. He remembered the wizened old black men in their threadbare suits standing behind the pulpit preaching about the promised land, and the rewards in heaven for those who followed the Word, but he'd never quite understand what it meant. He remembered, for example, that before word of Lincoln's emancipation of the slaves in Texas and the other rebellious states reached them in East Texas, preachers had talked about the need to be submissive and obedient, but after 1862, they talked of crossing Jordan, and finally being able to stand before the Throne of God as free men and women, the message, seeming to contradict what had gone before, confusing Ben's young mind, until he finally just shut it out. The messages from the black preachers, before and after emancipation, conflicted with what he'd heard white people say, especially the white Baptist and evangelical preachers who said that black people were descended from Noah's son, Ham, who, seeing his father drunk and naked in his tent, refused to cover him, and because of that act of disrespect, his descendants were cursed to forever be their brothers' servants. He'd believed this until his father showed him the passage in the Bible, Genesis 9. 20-27, that described how, after Ham's act of disrespect, Noah had cursed Ham's son, Canaan, and condemned him to be a slave to his brothers. In Ben's mind, that made a completely mockery of the whole 'Mark of Ham' nonsense.

He decided to take a chance and challenge Jeremiah.

"You ever think that sometimes you get it wrong?"

"Get what wrong?" Jeremiah blinked and looked confused. "You mean, get the Good Book wrong?"

Ben dipped his head in acknowledgment. "That's right. Not that it's wrong, but I think sometimes people misunderstand what it says."

"You sayin' I don't know my Bible, son of Ham?"

As a matter of fact, I am. "Well, you come close, but you don't get it exactly right."

"A plague on you, boy," Jeremiah thundered. "What don't I get right?"

Ben strained to remember the names before speaking. "Well, you keep talking about the Mark of Ham, and how that means black people supposed to be slaves," he said. "It wasn't Ham who was cursed, you know. It was his son, Canaan, and some folks use that to say that's why it was okay to make slaves of black folks, because it was Canaan who was black. Fact is, though, it was Canaan's brother, Cush, who was black, and he wasn't the one who was cursed. So, you see, it's not the Mark of Ham you should be talking about, but the Mark of Canaan, or if you want to talk about black folks, the Mark of Cush. You see what I mean?"

Jeremiah's brow wrinkled and he half closed his eyes. When he opened them again, they blazed. "That don't matter who was marked, boy. You are a cursed race. Now, we don't have slavery here in Eden, but that don't mean I consider you my equal, because you ain't. The biggest mistake was ever made was to bring you people to this country in the first place. We should've left you in Africa where you belong."

Ben shook his head. "You over two hundred years too late to wish for that. We been here for generations, and are just as much a part of this country as you. Considering how so much of it was built by the sweat of our labor, you could say, we're even more a part of this land than people like you."

He knew he was playing with fire, baiting the man like this, but part of him refused to hold back. He'd heard the pronouncements of inferiority and not belonging too long; had seen the white men treat the Indian, generations on the land the white man was taking away from him, treated as if he didn't belong; a rebellious streak him forced him to lash out.

Jeremiah reeled back in his chair as if he'd been struck. His lips quivered. "Without the white man, this land would be useless," he said, spittle dribbling freely with each word.

"The land was hardly useless. It had buffalo herds, and the white man killed most of 'em off. The Indians lived off the land, and the white man drove 'em off the best land. You cut down trees and plow up land, and then it dries out and the wind blows it away. What do you do? You move on and tear up the next piece of land. How is that making the land useful?"

"We don't do that here in Eden," Jeremiah said. "We protect the land."

Ben slapped his hand on the table, causing both Moses and Jeremiah to flinch. "So, you're not like most white men is what you're saying?"

"That's right."

"But, you look at me, and you see a colored man. You see me the same as every other colored man?"

Jeremiah's mouth opened and closed. His eyes

blinked rapidly. He closed his mouth and swallowed.

"Okay," he said. "So, you ain't like every other colored man. I'll grant you that, but it still don't make you my equal." He smiled. An evil smile that gave Ben a cold feeling in the pit of his stomach. "It ain't got nothin' to do with why we here now, though. It don't prove that Moses didn't betray Eden."

"It *does* prove it." Ben turned his attention to the jury. "If Moses led me and my soldiers to Eden, why didn't we show up right after he did? I'll tell you why. Because, we spotted him, and figured out that he was watching us. So, we let him go about his business, while we scouted the mountains looking for the trail of Mr. Heatherton and his people." He felt Moses tense up next to him. Nudging him lightly, he looked down and smiled. "When he started moving away from us, I had my best scout track him. I can promise you, he had no idea he was being followed. My man tracked him here, and came back and told me. That's why we're here.

He could see now that four of the women had lifted their heads and were watching him, hanging on his every word. The remaining two still had their heads down, but tilted in such a way that they could easily hear him.

"Now, you could say that, in a way, Moses led us here," he continued. "But, he certainly didn't do it willingly. In fact, my scout told me, he cut a trail through the mountains that anybody but an expert scout wouldn't have been able to follow. So, you see, he tried to make sure we *wouldn't* find Eden."

Jeremiah had been watching the women, too, and saw that they were listening to Ben's account.

"The soldier ain't tellin' you the whole story," he said. "I think Moses consorted with them. Remember, he had the smell of a camp fire on his clothes."

Ben knew that his next words were crucial. He would not, could not, tell an outright lie, but, he had to get them thinking in another direction.

"We found Mr. Heatherton's camp site," he said. "There were signs of a fire that hadn't been properly put out. I think when you left him there to watch, he sat near that fire to keep warm, until it died down. Wouldn't he get the smell of a fire from that?"

All six women's heads were bobbing up and down. Moses smiled up at Ben. "I did sit by the fire a spell," he said quietly, but loud enough that Jeremiah heard. "I know I shouldn't have done it, but it got so cold the first night."

"There you have it," Ben said to the jury. "The case against this boy is based on the smell of a camp fire in his clothes. You just heard how he could've gotten that smell, and it has nothing to do with us. I know you folks been living up here in these mountains, cut off from the rest of the country, for a long time. So, let me tell you how the court is supposed to work. If you got any doubt about a person's guilt, you have to find him not guilty. You have no concrete proof that this boy willingly led me and my soldiers here, and you have my word and his that he didn't. It appears to me that you have no choice but to find him not guilty."

Jeremiah frowned when he saw the six heads bobbing up and down.

"Come now, sisters," he said. "You can't be lettin' this spawn of Satan corrupt your minds like this. This is why we left the outside world in the first place; so that we could find a place of innocence. If you follow this man, you will be allowing the serpent into Eden once again."

The older of the six women, who appeared to Ben to be in her mid-forties, looked at Jeremiah. "But, Prophet," she said. "What he says makes sense. I've knowed Moses since he was born. I was the midwife what helped Sarah deliver him. He ain't never been nothin' but a good boy, who honors his father and mother. But, he is just a boy, 'n you left him out there all alone agin men who been to war. I jest can't see him doin' what you accuse him of doin'."

The other five women nodded as she spoke.

"I agree with Mary," the young woman sitting next to her said.

Jeremiah stood and pointed at the women. "You sayin' you find these two not guilty?"

The woman, Mary, stood, and though she trembled and her expression was fearful, she held Jeremiah's gaze. "Not jest, not guilty," she said. "We think they's innocent. Ain't gonna be no lashin' of neither of them."

"You're forgettin' your place, Mary. You're also forgettin' who been takin' care of this community for the past sixteen years."

Hands clasped at her waist, Mary looked from Jeremiah to Ben and back. "No, Jeremiah, I ain't forgettin' nothin'. I know you mean well, but I also know sometimes you kin be hard as flint, 'n you's stubborn as a mule."

Something like fear, or that's what it looked like to Ben, passed across Jeremiah's face.

"I only tried to do what was best for my people here. You know that better than anybody, Mary."

"I know you done tried, Jeremiah, I surely do. But, sometimes you need to stop and listen to other folks."

"No, Mary, folks need to listen to me. I done followed the good book, 'n tried to lead y'all onto the path of righteousness, 'n away from the iniquities of that mad world out there where this descendant of Ham come from."

"The world out there has changed a lot since you hid away up in these mountains," Ben said. "Sure, there's still a lot of bad, but there's a lot of good, too. One of the things is that now there are no more slaves. Nothing but free people, free to make mistakes and find their own way. You say you don't have slaves here in Eden, but that's wrong, you do have slaves." Ben waved his hand, taking in the jury, the armed men, and the women and children standing behind him. "You've enslaved all these people here sure as if you'd put chains on 'em. You've enslaved their minds, keeping them ignorant of the world outside this place, keeping them subject to your thoughts and wishes instead of their own."

"No, you're wrong. Everybody here's free. Eden is the only place in this country where everybody is free."

"If they're free, answer me this," Ben said. "Can they leave anytime they want?"

"Who would want to leave this for the troubles of the outside world?" For the first time, Jeremiah failed to make eye contact with Ben.

"You didn't answer my question. No need, though, I know the answer. Nobody's allowed to leave without your permission. You've set yourself up as a little king here, with everybody at your beck and call. I'm confused, though. If you hadn't kidnapped Mr. Heatherton and the others, this place might never have been found. Why'd you do that?"

Jeremiah's eyes blazed. "I don't have to tell you a thing, boy. I don't answer to you." His voice rose higher with each word. "I don't answer to nobody! Brother Micah, Brother Solomon, come up here and take these two for punishment." He pointed at Ben and Moses. "And, while you're at it, take Sister Mary, too. She needs to learn her place in the order of things here."

Nothing happened. Jeremiah looked around, his eyes wild. "Micah, Solomon, where are you?"

"They right here," George Toussaint said, as he stepped from the back of the nearest row of cabins. "But, they can't do what you ask."

Charles Ray

Chapter 23

Ben smiled at the sight of his second in command. Behind Toussaint he saw Layton and Hall, their carbines pointed at Jeremiah's gun men, now sitting on the ground with their hands resting on the tops of their heads.

"Well, George," he said. "You took your time getting here."

Toussaint shrugged and smiled. "Sorry, Ben, but we had to wait until everybody was payin' attention to you. Them two fellas that was standin' in front of you wasn't where we could reach at first, then they moved into the crowd. You couldn't see behind you, but looks like everybody was really hangin' on what you was sayin', and they was tryin' to get 'em to stop payin' attention. Say, I didn't know you could talk so pretty like that."

"Never mind that. Did you send someone to take care of those two guards in the back?"

"Yeah, Hightower and Tatum done took care of them." He pointed. Hightower led three men and a woman around the first row of cabins behind Jeremiah's, and behind him came Tatum, prodding the barrel of his carbine in the backs of two men in black with their arms high. "There they come now."

James Heatherton stepped up behind Toussaint, and when he saw the freed hostages, rushed past the milling crowd toward them. He embraced the older of the three men.

The two men walked up arm in arm, followed by the other three hostages, who looked around, blinking their eyes as if they'd just awoken from a dream. Hightower and Tatum shoved their two prisoners toward the other six men in black, who were kneeling on the ground.

"Sergeant Carter," James Hightower said. "Permit me to introduce my father, William Hightower."

The elder Heatherton was shorter than his son, and a bit soft in the middle, compared to the ascetic leanness of the younger man, and was dressed in brown nankeen trousers, a faded white shirt, and scuffed brown boots. His white hair, thinning on top, stuck out in all directions, and he peered at Ben over the gold rims of a pair of spectacles, looking nothing like the successful businessman his son had described him to be. Up close, though, Ben could see the family resemblance, the set of the nose, and a certain haughty look in the eyes.

"Well, sergeant," the elder man said. "On behalf of my colleagues, I do thank you." He stepped away from his son and turned, sweeping his hand to indicate his companions, a slender man of his height, with an oval face and black hair that hung over his forehead; a tall, broad-shouldered man whose flax-colored hair was combed straight back and hung over the frayed color of his blue cotton shirt, and a woman dressed in brown pants and shirt, wide of hip and narrow of shoulder, her brown hair pulled severely back and arranged in a bun, she had large, brown eyes and a slightly crooked nose. Her unpainted lips and long-fingered hands were as chapped as the men. The elder Heatherton stepped toward them, and placed a hand on the small man's shoulder. "This is Merriwether Johnson, my second in command," he said. "The big man's Henry Cabot. He's responsible for taking care of our horses and gear. And the lady is Cady Logan, my secretary, and the chronicler for our expedition. Folks, this is Sergeant Carter, who, according to my son, James, is here to rescue us."

The three mumbled and smiled at Ben and the soldiers, still looking dazed, except for Logan, who stepped forward and faced Ben with her hands on her hips.

"How did you find us?" she asked. "That tunnel through the mountain was pretty cleverly concealed."

Ben inclined his head toward Hightower. "Sergeant Hightower there is the best scout in the U.S. army, ma'am. He found it. They left a boy to look out for anyone looking for you, I suppose. We spotted him and followed him here."

"Quite enterprising of you," the elder Heatherton said. "And, lucky for us."

"Yes," Logan said. "That mad man's plans for us were . . . well, let's just say, I am glad you came along when you did."

"I don't understand why they took you," Ben said. "You were outside the valley, and like you said, you likely wouldn't have found the entrance."

"That's easy," Heatherton said. "They captured us to use as breeding stock

Chapter 24

After the shock of the old man's words wore off, Ben gathered him, his son, James, the woman, Mary, Moses, and his mother, Sarah, in front of Jeremiah's cabin. The prophet and his men had been secured with ropes and were under guard nearby. The six sat at Jeremiah's table, the tattered Bible still in the center.

"Now, Mr. Heatherton," Ben said. "Please explain what you meant about the four of you being used as breed stock."

"Well, the way he explained it, and you have to remember, I was a bit upset at the time, after being kidnapped, so I might not have gotten it all, is that they've been experiencing some problems with the latest batch of children born here, and Jeremiah thought they needed to introduce new blood."

Ben looked confused. "What kind of problems?"

"The last two babies were stillborn," Mary said. "Poor things came way too early, too."

"And, we had four who only lived a few weeks," said Sarah. "My last one was like that. It had problems breathing from the first, and finally, it just couldn't get enough air, 'n it died."

"You'll pardon me saying it, ma'am," Ben said. "But, you seem a bit old to be having babies." To Mary, he said, "And, you too. I hope I'm not insulting you by saying that."

Both women laughed. "No insult, sergeant," Mary

said. "You right. We both long past the time for birthin' babies, 'cept as midwives. But, The Prophet said we needed more people, 'n not enough of the girls have reached child-bearin' age, so we older women have to do our part."

The older Heatherton slapped the table. "It's unconscionable what that man was doing. Not only is it dangerous for the babies when women this age try to bear children, but it's dangerous for them as well. But, that, from what I gathered listening to people here talk, is not the worst problem. With just nine men, there's been a bit of inbreeding, and just like it happens with livestock, when you breed close kin, you have a lot of bad conditions cropping up. That's why he brought us here. He wanted to introduce variety into Eden's bloodlines."

Ben felt the bile of anger rising in his throat. He'd been too young when he and his family were slaves to be aware of what went on, but after emancipation, and after his mother's death, his father had told him what went on at some of the plantations; how the owners had bred their slaves like cattle, often forcing women to bear children when they were past safe child-bearing age, in order to increase the number of slave they owned.

His mission had been to rescue the kidnapped expedition members, but he could not ride away from what he'd learned. He couldn't be sure what laws the man Jeremiah had violated, that he would let the courts decide. He and the detachment would transport Jeremiah and the men to the sheriff in Cimarron. The women and children would also be transported. What would come of them, he didn't know. When he informed Mary and Sarah of his intentions, they insisted that they all must be kept together.

"Me 'n Sarah been together since 'fore Prophet Jeremiah brung us here," Mary said. "I reckon since we gonna have to leave here, we'd get by best if we stayed together, 'n took care of our young'uns together."

"What about the other women and children?" Ben asked.

"It'd probably be best if we all stayed together," she said. "Least ways, 'till we get used to bein' outside here."

Ben was accustomed to dealing with renegade Apaches and outlaws, even with errant soldiers, but this was completely unfamiliar territory. He had no idea what the authorities in Cimarron might do.

"I suppose something can be worked out," he said. To Heatherton, he said, "I reckon you'll be glad to get home."

The old man ran a hand through his unkempt hair. "Well, I will be glad to get out of this place, but I'd kinda like to do a little more exploring of this valley. We found some pottery shards just the other side of that tunnel they brought us through, and I believe the Anasazi might've once lived in this hidden valley."

James Heatherton leaned across the table and grasped his father's wrist. "Absolutely *not,* father," he said. "You are going home. Your explorations are over for a while."

"Aw, come on, boy, I'm pretty close to making a momentous discovery here."

"This valley's not going anywhere. We can come back in a few months, or even next year. In fact, if you'll agree to come home, I'll even come with you."

"You would? You'd really do that?"

"Of course, I would. I think I could let my foreman handle the mine's affairs for a few weeks."

"Son, you don't know how happy it makes me to hear you say that."

The younger Heatherton looked over the top of his father's head at Ben and smiled. "It's the only way I can keep an eye on you, and besides, why should you have all the adventure."

Charles Ray

Chapter 25

With people riding double, they were able to move the entire population of Eden to Cimarron, a journey that took five days. Their arrival in Cimarron caused quite a stir, but after William Heatherton explained what Jeremiah and his men had done, and described what he'd observed about life in Eden, the nine men were jailed, and the town's church ladies took charge of the women and children, settling them in with various families around the town, seeing that the younger children were enrolled in school, and the women and teens were found jobs.

The sheriff, a portly, bald man with a white mustache that draped down to the bottom of his chin, glared at Jeremiah as he turned the big key in the cell door's lock.

"You gonna be goin' away for a long time, old man," he said. "We jest got us a new judge in the court here, and he don't like cattle thieves or men who abuse women."

"God will provide for me," Jeremiah said. "For, I am one of his chosen."

"Yeah, you keep thinkin' that, old man, all the way to the territorial prison."

After ensuring that the nine prisoners were securely locked away, the sheriff took statements from Heatherton, Johnson, Cabot, Logan, and Ben. He informed them that the kidnapping alone would ensure that the nine would spend a long time in prison. As for the cult-like community that Jeremiah lorded over, he refused to even guess how the judge would react to that, or, after having talked to Mary, Sarah, and the others, if the women would even testify against him at a trial.

"I seen it before," he said. "White women what got took by the Injuns. After they done lived with 'em for long enough, they become part of the community, and they don't hate 'em for kidnappin' 'em and takin' 'em from they real homes. I'll be dog if I understand it, and I wouldn't believe it if I hadn't seen it with my own eyes."

Ben was familiar with that attitude. He'd seen it in Hightower, who, on the rare occasions when he spoke of the tribe that had taken him and his mother, he did so with a measure of affection.

"I just hope those poor women and children will be able to make a go of it," Ben said.

The sheriff ran a hand over his bald pate. "Ain't no way to tell. Some adjust, and some don't. It's the young'uns I worry about. They don't know no other life, so it's gonna be real hard for them."

"It'll help the way you folks reached out to help. Not many people would."

"Hell, sergeant, out here, we all got to pull together just to survive, but I reckon you already know how that is."

"I do, indeed," said Ben. "Anyway, thank you, sheriff. Me and my men will be departing today. We have to see Mr. Heatherton, here, and his people home safely, and then get back to Fort Union."

"Y'all have a good trip. I'll send a telegram when we need you to come back for the trial."

Chapter 26

They escorted the Heatherton party all the way home, declined an invitation to stay and hit the trail immediately for Fort Union, a two-day ride away.

That first evening, they set up camp in a clearing on the side of the road, twenty miles west of the town of Las Vegas.

Out of habit, Ben posted a sentry, assigning Corporal Reuben Kincaid first watch. He then squatted near the fire, sipping coffee given him by Corporal Marcus Scott, who had evening mess duty. Toussaint joined him at the fire, while the rest of the detachment sat around on tree stumps or saddles, waiting for the beans and pork, Scott was cooking to be ready.

Ben and Toussaint sat in silence for a long time, just watching the beans bubbling in the iron pot, and breathing in the aroma of beans and pork that hung in the air around the fire. Finally, Toussaint broke the silence.

"This was just about the strangest thing they done ever sent us to do," he said. "I mean, who'd of thought there'd be men hid up in them mountains with a, what do they call it in them stories you told me you read once—"

"A harem," Ben said. "The Arabian kings, they call 'em sheiks, had a lot of wives and concubines, and they kept 'em locked away in harems."

"Yeah, like one of them harems. I ain't never heard of such a thing."

149

"Lots of strange things in this world, George. I reckon there's even some stranger than this. But, you know, I learned something from it."

'Oh yeah, what's that?"

Ben took another sip of his now cooling coffee.

"When we first met Mr. Heatherton, the son, that is; I really didn't like him very much. I thought he acted kind of snooty, and was looking down on us."

"Yeah, I noticed you seemed a mite tense every time you was around him. 'Course, he did kinda have his nose in the air."

"True, but the longer he was around, the more I saw that he was just worried about his father, and that was his way of dealing with it."

"Okay, that make sense," Toussaint said. "So, what'd you learn from it?"

"You saw how that Jeremiah fella reacted to us because of our skin color, even the way Moses acted at first. When I went into that settlement, I could tell he didn't think I was a real threat. Well, he was wrong. I did the same thing with James Heatherton. I just assumed that his snooty ways was part of his personality; never stopped to consider he was worried about his pa." Ben paused and rubbed at his chin. "What I learned is that it's wrong to judge people based on first impressions. You got to get to know a person first, before you can decide what kind of person he is."

Toussaint chuckled. "Oh, that. I learned that lesson long, long time ago. In fact, I think it's 'bout the time you joined us for the first time. I thought you's this smart aleck, know-it-all, sergeant that thought he's better than the rest of us. Turned out I'se wrong. You ain't such a bad sergeant after all."

The two old friends shared a look for a few moments. Then, they started laughing.

A grouse in a nearby bush, startled by the sudden sound of laughter, squawked, and flew off toward the west in a flurry of flapping wings.

Books by this author:

The Buffalo Soldier series

Buffalo Soldier: Trial by Fire
Buffalo Soldier: Homecoming
Buffalo Soldier: Incident at Cactus Junction
Buffalo Soldier: Peacekeepers
Buffalo Soldier: Renegade
Buffalo Soldier: Escort Duty
Buffalo Soldier: Battle at Dead Man's Gulch
Buffalo Soldier: Yosemite
Buffalo Soldier: Comanchero
Buffalo Soldier: Range War
Buffalo Soldier: Mob Justice
Buffalo Soldier: Chasing Ghosts
Buffalo Soldier: The Piano
Buffalo Soldier: Family Feud
Buffalo Soldier: Lost Expedition

Al Pennyback mysteries

Color Me Dead
Memorial to the Dead
Deadline
Dead, White, and Blue
A Good Day to Die
The Day the Music Died
Die, Sinner
Deadly Intentions
Death by Design
Till Death Do Us Part
Deadly Dose
Dead Man's Cove

Dead Men Don't Answer
Deadly Paradise
Kiss of Death
Death in White Satin
Death and Taxis
Deadbeat
A Deadly Wind Blows
Death Wish
Deadly Vendetta
A Time to Kill, A Time to Die
Dead Ringer
Death of Innocence
Dead Reckoning
Murder on the Menu
Over My Dead Body
Bad Girls Don't Die

Ed Lazenby mysteries
Butterfly Effect
Coriolis Effect
The Cat in the Hatbox
Negative Side Effects
Murder is as Easy as ABC

Other fiction
Angel on His Shoulder
She's No Angel
Child of the Flame
Pip's Revenge
Wallace in Underland
Further Adventures of Wallace in Underland
Dead Letter and Other Tales

The White Dragons
The Dragon's Lair
Dragon Slayer
The Last Gunfighters
The Culling
Frontier Justice: Bass Reeves, Deputy
  U.S. Marshal
Angel on His Shoulder-Revised Edition
Battle at the Galactic Junkyard
Mountain Man
Devil's Lake
Vixen
Wagons West: Daniel's Journey
Wagons West: Trinity
Awakening
Fatal Encounters: The Adventures of Bass
  Reeves, Deputy U.S. Marshal

Nonfiction

Things I Learned from My Grandmother About
  Leadership and Life
Taking Charge: Effective Leadership for the
  Twenty-first Century
Grab the Brass ring
African Places: A Photographic Journey
  Through Zimbabwe and southern Africa
A Portrait of Africa
There's Always a Plan B
In the Line of Fire: American Diplomats in
  the Trenches
Advice for the Insecure Writer
Looking at Life Through My Lens
Ethical Dilemmas and the Practice of Diplomacy

Making America Grate Again
DC Street Art
Dead Letters and Other Tales: Revised edition

Children's books

The Yak and the Yeti
Samantha and the Bully
Molly Learns to Share
Where is Teddy?
Catie and Mister Hop-Hop
Tommy Learns to Count
Catie Goes to School

About the Author

Charles Ray has been writing fiction since his teens. He won a Sunday school magazine writing contest when he was thirteen, and having his byline on a short story published in a national publication forever hooked him on writing. During his time in the army (1962-1982) he often moonlighted as a newspaper or magazine journalist, and was the editorial cartoonist for the Spring Lake (NC) News, a weekly newspaper, during the 1970s. In addition to his writing, he was an artist/cartoonist and photographer for a number of publications, including Ebony, Eagle and Swan, and Essence, and had a monthly cartoon feature and did several covers for Buffalo, a now-defunct magazine that was dedicated to showcasing the contributions of African-Americans to the country's military history.

After retiring from the army, he joined the U.S. Foreign Service, and served as a diplomat in posts in Asia and Africa until his retirement in 2012. He has worked and traveled throughout the world (Antarctica is the only continent he hasn't visited), and now, as a full time writer, continues to globetrot looking for interesting things to write about, draw, or take pictures of.

A native of Texas, he now calls Maryland home. For more on his writing and other projects, check one of the following Web sites:

http://charlesaray.blogspot.com
http://charlieray45.wordpress.com
http://www.twitter.com/charlieray45

http://www.facebook.com/charlieray45
http://www.flickr.com/photos/charlesray45/
http://www.viewbug.com/member/charlesray

Author's photograph by Denise Ray-Wickersham

www.ingramcontent.com/pod-product-compliance
Lightning Source LLC
Chambersburg PA
CBHW060428130626
46555CB00005B/2263